Praise for *Growing Up on Route 66,* the first novel in this series:

"Lund presents an entertaining story of small town life - paperboys, the gentle aspects of life in a simpler time and the wonder of the people who make small towns the linchpin of America. Through the eyes of Mark Landon we find that the answers to the myriad questions of life and love aren't always easy to find."

--Bob Moore, *ROUTE 66 MAGAZINE* (Volume 9, Number 1; Winter 2001-02)

"If the trials of Kevin, Paul, and Winnie on the television show *The Wonder Years* remind you of your childhood, you'll enjoy this coming-of-age book. The author grew up in Rolla, and his characters, Mark Landon and Marcia Terrell, live in a small Missouri town along Route 66. The narrator tells funny stories of adolescence in the 1950s. As an adult, the narrator has a philosophical outlook. 'The road I've traveled has clearer landmarks when I look behind me than when I was moving forward.'"

--Tricia Mosser, *MISSOURI LIFE* (Volume 29, Number 6; December 2001)

Praise for *Route 66 Kids,* Lund's second novel:

"Babyboomers coming of age in a small Midwestern town on Route 66. It's a decade later but it reads like the 'Summer of '42.' An extremely heartwarming and nostalgic look at young people's angst during this age of wonder."

ROUTE 66 FEDERATION NEWS (Volume 9, Number 2; Spring, 2003)

"*Route 66 Kids*, follows the fortunes of his earlier hero and heroine of *Growing up on Route 66* , Mark Landon and Marcia Terrell, taking them through high school to the eve of Mark's departure for college at Southwest Missouri State College and Marcia's departure for . . . but you'll have to read the book to find out where Marcia is headed. . . . . No matter how often you've heard the phrase/title *You Can't Go Home Again*, Michael Lund's book convinces us that Thomas Wolfe was wrong. You can go home again, and *Route 66 Kids* takes us home wherever home was."

--William Frank, *FARMVILLE (VA) HERALD*, May 31, 2002,

Praise for *A Left-Hander on Route 66* Lund's third Novel:

"[*Left-hander*] is a howl with just enough of the serious to add contrast and spice."

--William Hoffman, award-winning author of *Godfires, Tidewater Blood*, and many more

Praise for *Miss Route 66* Lund's fourth Novel:

"'[W]hen do the girls get a book?' Well, here it is! *Miss Route 66* is the story . . . of Susan Bell (now Mrs. Susan Bell Thornton) of the famous Fairfield Circle and her foray into the teen-age world of beauty pageants, necking sessions, dating in the quaint world of the 50s and 60s when a girl waited for the phone to ring and didn't dare call a boy on her own."

--William Frank, *Farmville (VA) Herald*, February 18, 2004.

mother called you in to wash up and go to bed, when you were playing a leisurely game of kick-the-can and wished that the game could just go on and on. Fortunately, Lund promises that it will go on, in the second book in his series, *Route 66 Kids*, and, I hope, many more to come."

--Eric Kraft, author of *The Personal History, Adventures, Experiences & Observations of Peter Leroy*

Route 66 Spring

By

Michael Lund

BeachHouse Books

Chesterfield, Missouri, USA

Copyright

Graphics Credits:

Cover by Loren Robertson
Publication date July, 2004
ISBN 1-888725- 98-2   Regular print BeachHouse Books Edition

Library of Congress Cataloging-in-Publication Data
Lund, Michael, 1945-
  Route 66 spring / by Michael Lund.
     p. cm.
  Includes bibliographical references and index.
  ISBN 1-888725-98-2 (alk. paper) -- ISBN 1-888725-99-0 (large type macroprintbooks : alk. paper)
  1. United States Highway 66--Fiction. 2. Poor families--Fiction. 3. Missouri--Fiction. I. Title.
  PS3562.U486R683 2004
  813'.54--dc22

www.beachhousebooks.com

an Imprint of
𝔖cience & 𝔥umanities 𝔓ress
PO Box 7151
Chesterfield, MO 63006-7151
(636) 394-4950
beachhousebooks.com

Route 66 Spring

Michael Lund

For Bill Frank, who knows the landscape
of Missouri and of the human heart.

ACKNOWLEDGMENTS

Again, I must thank the family, friends, and students who have listened to or read early versions of my stories. Their responses--sometimes praise, sometimes censure--have helped me immeasurably in the subsequent shaping of material into fiction.

I am especially grateful to Susan Stinson and Jim Shifflett for editorial suggestions in the preparation of this manuscript. And I wish to acknowledge my continuing gratitude to Dr. Bud Banis, my publisher, for his commitment to the concept of this series, for his generosity, and for his friendship.

For information about the Missouri landscape, I have consulted Thomas R. *Beveridge's Geological Wonders and Curiosities of Missouri*, second edition, revised by Jerry D. Vineyard (Rolla, Missouri: Missouri Department of Natural Resources, Division of Geology and Land Survey, 1990) and *Springs of Missouri* by Jerry D. Vineyard and Gerald L. Feder with Sections of Fauna and Flora by William L. Pflieger and Robert G. Lipscomb (Rolla, Missouri: Missouri Geological Survey and Water Resources, 1974).

Any errors in fact or inconsistencies of narration in the pages that follow are attributable solely to the author.

Route 66 Spring

Michael Lund

Prologue: Missouri Legends

I

The Sinkhole Lovers are a touchstone of history for the Show Me State, a story told and retold by generations of Missourians. In this legend a young, star-crossed couple--we don't even have their names--were so desperate to be together they asked the earth to swallow them up rather than let their families keep them apart. And it did. Gu-ulp!

There are different versions of this tale, of course, and its setting is a matter of some disagreement. St. Louis County, St. Genevieve County, and Phipps County at least have claimed to be the location where the lovers dropped, quite literally, out of sight. All are famous for sinkholes, created by the carving of underground streams in vast karst areas. And it's a sudden, large cave-in that has always explained the lovers' vanishing.

Only recently, however, has a new aspect of this story come to the surface (so to speak!)--the sex factor.

You see, when the event originally occurred (or, for the cynics, when the fable was first concocted), late in the nineteenth century, the physical life of lovers was never directly discussed in polite society. One might talk in general terms about "courtship," "the wedding night," "conception," but with none of the concrete details included. The body beneath a "heaving bosom" or "broad shoulders" existed only by inference, not in graphic representation.

During the turbulent 1960s, however, such old taboos were exploded, and a new frankness characterized the language of rebellious youth. Formerly "private" body parts appeared in public print and photo, often with startling distinctness in terms of size, shape, tone, and resiliency.

Later, when those 1960s rebellious youths had grown into politically powerful babyboomers, they assumed control of American language. The abandonment of restraint they initiated could, apparently, only continue, especially as popular culture rewarded every new unveiling of reality, each more shocking term and concept. Eventually mainstream culture--television, movies, the internet--came to allow open discussion of all sexual matters. So the hoary legend of the Sinkhole Lovers is being repeated to the children of the new millennium with some bizarre twists.

It helps, however, to recall the old version first and then rethink that early tale within the latest framework. What we'll be doing shortly, then, is filling in (below the waists, so to speak) the portraits of two Victorian-era lovers.

A preface concerning the creation of sinkholes is necessary. The soft dolomite and limestone of Missouri's geology dissolves (relatively) easily in water. So, rain that falls in shut-in valleys finds ways to sink underground. And that water continues to eat its way underground to places of lower elevation, eventually emerging as a spring turning into a creek merging with other streams to become a river on its way to the sea.

Traveling beneath the surface, often for miles, the water dissolves additional surrounding rock. In places, open caverns are created underground. The earth and rock above can eventually fall into such spaces, leaving a sinkhole at the surface, an often neatly circular depression in the landscape. Water, of course, continues to gather in that sinkhole, join the underground flow of water, and begin the whole process again.

Now, let's consider the Sinkhole Lovers. To lend the story more immediacy we'll give hero and heroine names, William and Marie. Recognizing that their history has been told with a number of variations over the years, this will be a minor elaboration on the essential situation. In nearly all the versions, the man is of British descent, the woman French. Early Missouri was, of course, settled by both those peoples, though Spanish explorers had preceded them and later a sizable German influx occurred.

Anyway, the cultural chasm between William's and Marie's peoples is a first factor antagonistic to their union. Separated by the English channel in the Old World, the English and French had traditionally been at odds, if not (as they were in the early nineteenth century) at war. And that opposition continued in the battle for dominance of the New World.

Our romantic couple's families were also separated by religion (Protestant/Catholic), by landscape (their two farms were on opposite sides of a mountain), and by politics (like regions of their state before the Civil War, which were alternately slave and free). So their courtship did not grow out of childhood association, but instead began in a chance meeting at a stagecoach tavern near a major intersection of country-crossing roads.

William was accompanying an older cousin on a business trip to the north, Marie traveling west with a friend from school on their way to a country dance. Bad weather delayed each journey, and it was love at first sight, so profound neither questioned the other about family, background, commitments. By the time they learned, several days later, that they were members of warring camps, it was too late to imagine a future apart.

Innocently announcing their new attachment, they were stunned at the violence of their parents' reaction. They were forbidden ever to see each other, let alone marry, have children, grow old together, as they had intended.

Marie's maid secretly carried a message for William to meet his beloved one night at her favorite hideaway, a sunken dell on the far edge of her family's farm. They were to run away together, uniting the warring clans in their love. Neither realized that at the center of the small valley was a sinkhole, a depression caused where bedrock has been eroded by underground water. They were also pursued by members of both families.

Wrapped in each other's arms at the lowest point in the dell, they are surrounded by angry relatives and enemies. Standing tall in the light of a dozen torches, William declares boldly. "Do not attempt to come between us. We belong together."

"I love him," Marie tells her father. "It is our destiny never to be parted."

When the others advance, she calls out, "May God and this holy place preserve us!"

With a deep rumble the ground opens up, and the couple drop from sight. They fall feet first into a gaping hole in the earth's surface, a giant mouth. Gulp!

Descending with ropes into the chasm the next day, no one could find any trace of the Sinkhole Lovers. A few versions of the legend conclude that they emerged in another place and lived happy lives together, but most end the tale tragically in the bowels of the earth. The newest versions take, as has been indicated, a different tact. They open up a subject hidden in the story's early telling, the element of sex.

In this reinterpretation, William and Marie had not only fallen in love at first sight, but jumped into bed at the first opportunity, in that tavern near an intersection. And they were later caught in the woods, not praying for the blessings of God, but with his pants down and her dress up.

What the pursuing families saw in the light of a dozen torches were humans as God had made them. And they were more shocked at that exposure than the fact of their being together. The most outrageous telling suggests that it was the size, shape, tone, and resiliency of the young couple's sexuality that most offended the older observers! The elders' fierce moral code led them to call upon the earth to swallow up these transgressors of holy law--gu-ulp!

A more likely explanation is that the young couple, suddenly exposed, reached down to pull anything up and cover themselves--something akin to a giant fig leaf. So rather than dropping into the earth, they pulled the earth up around themselves. In either case, of course, love is thwarted, a story ended.

What occurs in the chapters that follow, though, is in many ways a continuation of, or perhaps a reworking of the Sinkhole Lovers' story. The immediate setting is the present, but the main action occurs in the late 1950s/early 1960s, that time of transition for America, after World War II and before the Sexual Revolution. The dreams of a group of young people were being swallowed, not by Mother Nature, but by what President Dwight Eisenhower called at the time "the Military-Industrial Complex." Gu-ulp! It remains to be seen if they can escape from the hole into which they are falling.

Janet's Story 1: Message in a Bottle

I have no doubt about when things began for me. They began with the bottle rising from the depths of Route 66 Spring. The glass artifact made an audible "plink" as it broke the surface, a soft announcement of its arrival within the steady bubbling of water pushing upward and the light splashes of the resulting stream flowing over rocks down into the valley.

Of course, this wasn't even called "Route 66 Spring" then. Its identity as an attraction along the Mother Road was some years in the future at that point. This was just the spring in the woods off a gravel road southwest of my home town, Fairfield, Missouri. A lot of kids used to hike out there on weekends or holidays, both because the spring was out of parents' reach and because it was such a beautiful, hidden spot. I had come this particular time to get away from Brad Whitaker.

The spring was quietly secluded from humans and their doings. A path wound from a decaying farmhouse several hundred yards through cedar and pine down from the ridge to which the road ran. The spring was up under a rock overhang at the bottom of the ridge, fifty feet of limestone cliff rising straight up above it. Dense hardwood made a semicircle against the cliff's base, and this setting blocked out distant sounds.

Route 66 Spring wasn't famous as a site of miracle then either. The apparition of Sacagawea from the water's winter mists--just in time to save an Osage woman from probable death--was, if it had occurred at all, years in the past, but unknown to most who lived in these parts. No, this natural wonder was hidden from fame and interest at this, my own time of crisis.

Our state's soft rock makes it a land of geological wonders. Missouri is honeycombed with caves, for instance, its limestone and dolomite penetrated and hollowed out by water over the millennia. The region also features spectacular sink holes, circular depressions ten or twenty yards wide that pockmark fields and bottom land. And we have shut-ins, narrow valleys in which small rivers are constricted and sometimes seem to dive beneath a surface of jumbled rock.

But there are especially springs, small ones and large ones from which clear, clean water issues in all seasons of the year--Meramec Spring, Bennett Spring, Round Spring, Alley Spring, and dozens

8

more in the southern third of the state. Underground rivers, fed by rain water making its way through layers of soil and rock, feed rising currents that emerge as springs in the long valleys banked by high Ozark ridges.

There are many stories of strange things coming to the surface of the Show Me State's countless springs, having traveled who knows how many miles and years underground: dead fish from a species long thought to have been extinct; a towel left at a picnic at the other end of the state and washed into the local drainage system; a boy's homemade toy boat that got away from him on the neighborhood creek half a dozen years earlier.

But my bottle with the message might turn out to be the most famous of all magical appearances in a Missouri spring. The handwritten letter kept dry inside for fifty years changed my life and may well be responsible for improving the quality of life of unborn children well into the future. Until now, though, only I have known the full import of the message in the bottle. The time has come to tell its story.

When the bottle appeared, all I thought I had, as I fished it out with a forked stick pulled from the brush, was a summer day's discovery, a finder's-keeper I would show my college friends. Encrusted with mineral deposit and a goodly layer of slime, it had only vaguely a recognizable bottle shape. But I thought I saw what could be a cork at the narrow end, a stopper that suggested to me something might still be inside.

Anything to take my mind off Brad that day! He was pressuring me to marry him. We'd grown up together, dated in high school, and assumed ourselves naturally suited to a conventional life together. He had the support of both families and, until recently, my lukewarm acceptance of his uninspired proposal.

But coming home for the summer from college after my sophomore year, I'd looked at his solid build, his earnest face, his steady progress toward managing the family's prosperous insurance company and began to wonder what in the world I'd seen in him! He was kind but dull. He needed a wife to match.

"Honey," he had said to me the night before. "Honey, you don't need to go back to school in the fall. Let's get married this summer." We were parked in little pull-off along Lover's Lane. The bushes were thick, and no one else was in sight.

"I need to finish college," I pointed out, "if I'm going to get a job."

I was majoring in history, with the vague notion of teaching high school. The frontier was my favorite subject. I got excited about the challenges and opportunities people faced as America spread itself across the continent, those men and women in covered wagons crossing the prairies. Our own fates are shaped by such distant events in the past.

"I don't want to drive up to Columbia every weekend to see you," he complained. "Let's try to talk this out."

Frankly, I wasn't all that interested in talking at this point. We'd been necking for half an hour and I was starting to ache. Couldn't he do something more?

"I'm part of the firm now," he continued. We'd been at his graduation the weekend before, and he'd gone to work in Fairfield the next Monday. "I'll get a good salary. You won't ever need to work. We'll be raising a family."

We won't be raising a family if he doesn't figure out how to make love! Listening to the other girls at Stephens this year, I'd come to the conclusion it was past time for me to lose my virginity. From the stories they told me, all a boy needed was for a girl not to say no. I was being careful not to say no. What was holding Brad back?

"Put your hand here," I whispered and shifted him around.

"Honey, you know I shouldn't do that."

We should do that and more, I thought. Get excited!

But getting excited was something Brad did rarely, my steady-as-a-rock boyfriend/would-be husband. He didn't get excited about school, or his job, or the sweet young package he had in his arms. He just wanted to tie things down, get his immediate surroundings securely in place for a predictable, sure future.

I wanted him to take me to the back seat of the car and satisfy the rising fire of my desire. I ground my hips after his retreating hand, arched my neck to return to his lips, gasped for air like a drowning person. If he'd just push up against me I'd be at least as happy as when I rolled around on my dormitory bed with Miss Blue (a backrest with arms you put at the head of the bed). But Brad got away from me.

The day after this debacle I held in my hands a crusty old bottle, cold in the spring's water, a talisman from another age. Standing up at the edge of the bubbling pool, I shook it dry. And felt something knocking dully against the inside.

Patting the pockets of my jeans, I searched for a tool to open the bottle with, a handkerchief to wrap around the stopper and twist, or a jackknife to pry it open. It was sealed tight.

Decades later, I sometimes wonder if I didn't draw this talisman out of the earth's deep rather than stand there innocently as it broke into the air. So keen were my desires and so limited my hopes at that time that I might have willed it to the surface, calling it forth to save me from another day in a life of tedium.

I do believe, in fact, in long hidden forces emerging into the present, secrets of the past saving themselves for the future, days of fulfillment. My own destiny had been brewing under ground before that day, perhaps for years, unseen by anyone, least of all by me. But the bottle and the message changed everything. What I was to do with my life was inspired by what I read on the seventy-five-years-old papers and by the miracle of their finding.

"My Letter to an Unknown Friend" the manuscript was entitled. It was signed, "a woman who lost an entire world." This was the call to my true destiny. I knew it when I saw it. Goodbye, Brad. Hello, another life.

Louis's Story I: Well-Finding

When Bobby Green pointed to a spot on the ground in that farm yard deep in the Ozarks, I realized I'd been looking for the wrong thing all along.

Of course, I was only a boy then, still in college, so my life's searching didn't have so long a history at that point. And now, decades later, I can see that moment as one of many turning points, not the goal I'd been focused on since my father's early death. But it was a turn in the right direction.

I'd come to the farm by a circuitous route and the directions of a country store owner.

"So . . . so," I had asked little Mrs. Green of Green's Store several hours earlier, "So, I go down Tom's Creek Road . . . how far?" I know my brow was wrinkled in concentration, but I tried to keep a smile in front of my potential helpmate.

"'Bout--oh, I'd say--'bout three miles." It didn't sound right. I'd looked at the map, and this didn't fit. And incongruously, a part of me was thinking about another puzzle at the same time I listened to Mrs. Green: how to navigate through the Victorian underwear of my teenage sweetheart.

"Cross a little, and then a big creek," continued my present informant. "The big one has a cement spillway." (She said "*see*-ment.") "Then there's a

13

road goes off up to the left, quarter mile." I nodded, trying to follow in my head the maze of blue and brown lines on the United States Geological Survey map, which lay spread out on the seat of my state car.

I wished there was a map through my girlfriend's many layers of clothing, but I knew no such printed guide existed. I'd been frustrated almost to the point of tears last Friday night when I'd finally gotten Linda Forrester alone in the back seat of the family's 1952 Studebaker, "Smoky Joe." I was baffled at the fold after fold of material that lay between me and my goal. And Linda could not or would not help me.

I was that summer--and had been the previous summer--a well-finder, three-month employee of the Missouri Geological Survey. My job from June to August (when I wasn't studying engineering at the University of Missouri) involved tracking down well-drilling locations at the rate of about forty per week. And I was on the trail of a tough one, the one Bobby Green would finally point to--and thereby point me in a new direction as well.

In the back of my mind, though, I was also trying to figure out how to "go all the way" with the high school sweetheart I felt owed me for my faithfulness. We had dated during my senior year and then continued our relationship mostly by mail for the two years I was away at college. The much talked-about sexual revolution was remote to us, a conservative couple of the Heartland. Still, I felt it was time for me to achieve manhood.

"Left?" I said to Mrs. Green. "OK." I had learned it was good to repeat key turning points in the

14

directions provided by locals. Not only did it show them I was listening, paying attention, but I also knew from experience that even lifelong residents could get themselves turned around trying to be nice to the "college boy." Too eager to help, they might say "left" when they meant "right," thinking of coming from the other direction. They could point north when they were looking south, or speak about going up when they knew anyone had to drive downhill from that spot. So I tried to prompt review and keep track of everything that was said in the order in which it was given.

I knew I was a good tracker, a skillful detective in this job of well-finding. There was a well out there hiding, in a sense, from me. But the clues were also there, and I would follow them relentlessly to the correct location.

This elderly storekeeper, a key source of information in my hunt, spoke confidently. And the gaze through her wire-rimmed glasses went straight to my eyes. "Um-hm, left. Quarter mile."

Mrs. Green had folded her hands across her faded cotton dress when I came in. Now she was pointing, gesturing with a shake of a thin, pale hand. "It goes along a fenceline, little field. You can see it. Ain't nobody else back there. Just him. Though I've not been there myself." The "him" she referred to was a Mr. Carter, who'd had the well drilled years ago. I was surprised to learn he was still alive, still at the same location.

"You've not been there, to the Carter place?" I asked. Directions obtained by hearsay, second or third hand, often meant trouble. I thought for a moment that I might have to postpone this search, move on for now to an easier one.

My search for Linda's womanhood had already been postponed, though it had seemed easy enough earlier in the year. At that time kisses had led to full embraces and to my hand on one breast--well, my hand on at least the sweater that lay over the blouse covering a slip which protected a brassiere hiding the breast.

I had been reminded that much lay between me and my objective over the Christmas break, when I'd taken Linda out several times and pressed the rights of an established boyfriend. I'd been so tangled in her clothes when I finally approached bare skin on New Year's Eve in the pantry off her family's kitchen (everyone else was at the television waiting for the ball to drop on Time's Square) that I hardly knew what I'd found.

Still, I understood that my movement through clothes was an elaborate ritual of the age, the conservative 1950s and early '60s. Although Linda could offer little help, each successive unveiling was an accepted step in a mutual process, ending, of course, in engagement and marriage, a lifetime together.

The Survey's long-term interest in well locations was knowledge of Missouri's underground--soil, rock, water tables--through study of core samples taken during drilling. This well-finder's goal in mapping female dress in the era of Dwight Eisenhower was that Biblical "knowing" I'd imagined myself having for over a decade. My more immediate object this day in June was a well drilled nearly fifty years ago in the neighborhood of Lost Spring, Missouri, deep in rural Arkansas County.

Mrs. Green ran a country store at the crossing of state highway JJ and an unmarked gravel road, where I had arrived at 1:35, my second stop after lunch and an initial elevation check. At 1:15 I had logged my first well, which had been drilled for a new house only three years earlier. It was no trouble to find, the well-driller's terse directions scribbled on the white survey slip ("Miller--eight tenths of a mile south of Lost Spring on JJ") leading me directly to the Millers' place.

"Everybody knows where Carter lives," explained Mrs. Green. "He was born there, in the last century even. He don't come out much either."

"Well, thank you. Thank you very much," I said, knowing that politeness here would help me throughout the week. I had come up on this little country store, always a good place to get information, less than a mile past the Millers' on JJ. And the spry old woman--I assumed she was Mrs. Green from the sign above the door, "Green's Store"--had been eager to help. The next house I was searching for (and the well drilled at that location nearly half a century ago) was, according to this new friend, down the gravel road, "yonder."

"What you want old Carter for, anyway?" asked Mrs. Green, as I pulled open the store's screen door and stepped onto the sagging wooden porch. I turned back to explain how most well-drillers routinely notified the Survey when they finished new wells. And the Survey wanted to know, "for the record," the exact location.

I was careful not to give all the details of this operation, like the fact that I would also take an elevation reading. Explaining too much could worry these rural people who were always leery of the government, suspecting city folk of elaborate conspiracies. ("What you want to know that for, anyways?") And these conversations could go on too long, keeping me from making the schedule that drove my workday. (It was now 1:45.)

Mrs. Green, fortunately, did not seem to be alarmed that I wanted to know such things. "You be careful driving, now," she concluded. "These gravel roads can fool you. That flint will flat your tires if you go too fast."

"OK. I sure will. Thanks again." It would not be a flat tire that stopped me in my tracks that day, but the life-changing discovery that I'd been seeking the wrong thing all along.

Janet's Story II: Waiting

My husband has often told me--and others have concurred--that I have a distinctive laugh. It's not an explosion, some sudden burst of exhilaration. Nor is it a racking belly laugh, the kind that goes on and on, leaving you exhausted and weeping. No, my laugh begins, he claims, softly somewhere deep inside, rises through a moderate, lengthy crescendo, and arrives at a satisfied, sustained conclusion--hoo-hoo, ho-ho, hee-hee, haaaaah.

I'm a tall woman for my generation at five foot ten, but I've always been slender. After many years of use, this old body is a bit stooped. But people still tell me that my laugh travels a long way before it reaches the open air.

It pleases my husband that I often chuckle while we are making love, but it certainly didn't suit the first man I slept with. I pressured poor Brad Whitaker into taking my virginity before I dumped him. (I know. This was not such a nice thing to do. But there were supposed to be benefits for him as well as for me in this coupling!) I had coaxed him into the back seat of his father's new Ford Galaxy two nights after the afternoon in which I found my bottle in the spring.

I had worked that day--as I had for several summers in high school and college--as a receptionist in my father's office. He was what we called in those days simply "a doctor," but now we would call it a "family practice." My tasks were simple--help patients sign in, find their charts, direct them from the outer office to one of our three examining rooms. My mother took payment and handed out insurance forms in a small alcove off the main waiting room. Nurse Riley assisted my father in treating patients.

My routine was boring beyond belief. Nothing momentous waited at the end of this tedious process, only the assurance that it was all to be repeated the next day and the next.

I did what I could to liven things up, of course, especially on slow days: talked to the fish in the aquarium (little response there); sang to the plants (perhaps they would have done better without my care); read books within books (that is, I hid racy titles inside literary classics). But the days were long.

Now that I think back on it, I, just like the patients, might have been waiting in the waiting room. I hoped that this wasn't what I would do with my life, that some other destiny was on its way to me. I didn't have the slightest notion of what that different fate could be. Sainthood as in Joan of Arc, genius as in Madame Currie, royalty as with Grace of Monaco didn't seem likely for such a small-town, pretty (I was told), but not especially brilliant (I was told that as well) girl. What could I be?

My fantasies consisted more of vague situations than specific events: a man's arms wrapped me in a warm embrace; I gave orders that others were eager to carry out; some ominous force, an agent of destruction, threatened everything I had worked for. I suspect such daydreams were not unique to me.

20

Many young girls strained against the limited future offered them in these years. But we didn't know what we really wanted.

Brad was sure I wanted to be Mrs. Whitaker.

Only Sophie Anderson seemed to think I might need anything different. She was one of the rare agents of excitement in my receptionist's daily routine.

Probably a hypochondriac, she came to see my father at least once a week with some complaint or other: stiffness in the lower back; excessive congestion; unsettled bowels. Of course, at nearly 100 years of age, she had reason to believe herself failing. Still, she drove the three blocks from her house to his office in her own car and acted as if her mission was to help me and the other patients while she was here.

"Janet, I want to listen to your heart," she announced one day near my tryst with Brad.

"My heart?" I giggled. She was leaning on a cane beside my receptionist's desk, a halo of silver hair around a smile. Her eyes were bright, her interest genuine.

"Go get me your father's stethoscope. I want to listen to your heart."

"I think it's fine, Mrs. Anderson. My dad keeps an eye on those things."

"Oh, Janet, a man doesn't know."

I gestured toward one of the chairs beside the aquarium, intimating that she should just sit and wait her turn like the other patients.

"I can't use his equipment, Mrs. Anderson. And besides, he's in with Mr. Dolamar. Now, let's just wait until the doctor is ready to see you."

"I'll take your pulse," she insisted, putting her hand on my wrist. I turned my hand palm up so she could rest her fingertips on the right spot. Her other hand still gripped her cane.

"Ah, a strong pulse, a steady one. I think I'm feeling something. Hold still, now."

Mrs. Anderson wasn't exactly a fortuneteller, but she did believe she could sometimes see things when she touched another person or held someone's intimate possession. She was so old and had known so many people that I liked her accounts of the past and predictions of the future, even if they were fantasy.

"What do you see, Mrs. Anderson?"

"It's a stream, no, a river, honey. Your life will be lived on the water. I see it now. A beautiful river, clean water flowing."

Well, the blood in my pulse could certainly suggest current in a stream, so I wasn't shocked at her assumptions. And there were plenty of rivers in Missouri.

"Is it the ocean? Am I going on a long journey??

"Oh, no child, but something's coming to you. No, it's come to you from far away. A story."

That sent a little chill down my spine. I did have a story from long ago, the papers in the bottle.

"What's it about? Who's it from?"

"It's not a prince, honey, not your Prince Charming. It's . . . it's . . . ."

22

"What?"

Mrs. Anderson looked back over her shoulder, leaned down close to my ear, and whispered: "It's the course of true love!"

And that started my laugh. What a sweet old lady!

It was that same laugh, issuing from the back seat of Brad's father's Galaxy, that so undid the man who thought he was my true love. He'd given in to my seduction when I got his belt undone and his zipper down.

I didn't know how all this was going to go, of course, having heard only the expurgated versions of deflowering narrated by my fellow students at Stephens College. Many were cloaked in an alcoholic haze and were probably mostly fiction, anyway. No matter what the truth was, though, I wanted to get on with it--with passion, with sex, with adult life.

I hadn't really thought about the possibility that it might be Brad's first time too. Brad's astonishment at his own body made me laugh.

I guess there was some discomfort for me at first, though, to tell the truth, I was so pleased to have gotten this business under way at last that I wasn't shocked or put off by any pain. Very quickly, Brad was comfortably where I thought he was supposed to be, and it was starting to feel rather nice for me. I assumed he was perfectly satisfied with his accomplishment.

Then this terrible quivering began. Brad's head lifted up off my shoulder. His eyes went wide in astonishment, and his mouth popped open. A piece of gum he'd rather artfully kept tucked away

23

through the preliminary rounds of kissing dropped unceremoniously onto the tip of my nose and stayed there.

I couldn't help it. A laugh started so low in my insides it might have come from my womb. And its gentle shaking was transmitted to Brad, whose system had risen to a point of excitement just short of release. So it released and he cried out and I laughed. Hoo-hoo, ho-ho, hee-hee, haaaaah . . . .

That night I read again the message in the bottle and knew I had to do something different with myself.

Louis's Story II: The View from Walnut Ridge

I got in the state car, backed away from the store front, started down Tom's Creek Road. I should have checked Mrs. Green's directions against a topographical map again, but I needed to keep moving. Time would be tight as it was.

I knew about the flint Mrs. Green had warned me against, as nearly every week found me changing a tire by the side of some country lane. But I couldn't go slow just because of that possibility.

My job was to find both a well's location and the elevation at that site. Geologists back at the Survey wanted to gauge the well's placement in the context of adjacent features like roads and buildings, but also among things above and below it, neighboring hills and valleys. They were mapping up and down, that is, as well as back and forth.

Well-finders worked generally by counties, carrying from Survey headquarters in Fairfield the relevant county road maps, section topographical maps, and a bundle of small white slips of paper that identified all the wells drilled since the last well-finder had come through. For several decades well-finders had been college students working summers, though at one time there had been at least one full-time employee assigned to the project. The county I was working today was miles from any real town, almost a wilderness spotted by tiny villages like the appropriately named Lost Spring.

Driving, I tried to chart in my mind what I had felt the previous weekend as I'd slid a hand along Linda's skirt, but it wasn't easy. This neo-Victorian age had a great fear of the body, and the clothes that hid nature's secrets were themselves kept mysterious.

I had studied what I could, including the womanswear section of the family Sears Catalog, that compendium of all things necessary to middle-class life. But the perfect feminine forms there looked more like mannequins than live models. And the unwrinkled, pure white, ideally shaped items of dress didn't match the reality I'd felt of bunched material here, rough clasp there, protruding strap and frayed seam. Linda didn't wear what I saw on these pages (let alone centerfold) of *Playboy*, at the time still modest in its poses and made even more discrete by the airbrush.

Ten minutes later I passed a place that looked right: a two-lane gravel driveway curved off, but to the right, not the left. And it was before the spillway over a creek, not after. I drove on another mile, then two. But nothing looked good. The road rose to the top of a ridge, and I could see the yellow gravel snaking out ahead of me along the high ground.

There was a place to pull off. The topographical map showed me now at Walnut Ridge, but none of the structures (marked on the map by small black squares) along the gravel road I had just driven matched the houses and old barns visible from this spot. Still, the map could be in error, probably drawn from aerial photographs and verified (in theory) by a field team. Sometimes they missed things. I would have to go back.

The view from Walnut Ridge was stunning, I know, though my immature mind recorded it only faintly in an almost subconscious way: June sunshine lighting every tree in the Ozark valley. A stretch of Bryant's Creek, eventual tributary to the rushing White River, wound invisibly but audibly through the virgin hardwood. Even though I'd passed courses in geology and botany, I had no real capacity to enjoy woods or water yet.

Tossing the county road map down on the front seat, I put the car into gear and stepped on the gas. The '57 Chevy spun its rear wheels in the loose gravel and then tore down the hillside. I had stopped only long enough to study the best route back to my bench mark. I had already lost one well (Carter) on this swing, and I didn't want to lose another (Miller).

The problem was the altimeter I used to record elevations at well sites, the same kind used in airplanes: it would have drifted in time. The altimeter was sensitive to air pressure: the higher it went, the more a thin metal membrane was pushed out by an expanding core of gas. A needle registered the height, from sea level to 5,000 feet, on a circular face under glass.

But the altimeter reacted also to changes in the weather, to arriving fronts of low or high pressure. So, standard well-finding practice required me to check the reading at a known elevation (a bench mark installed by the U.S. Geological Survey) every hour. Then a simple algebraic formula would proportion the drift over time, adjusting readings for fixed moments within the hour: E^2[levation] - E^1 / T^2 [ime] - T^1 = R[atio of feet / minute change in elevation].

Time had also been a factor in my date with Linda the previous weekend. I had decided to lose my virginity by the end of the summer preceding my junior year of college, and that meant I should make progress on each date with Linda. The country club dance had ended at 10:30, and I had to have her back home by midnight (actually a rather liberal curfew for the times). I had only an hour and fifteen minutes to advance on my goal once I pulled into my favorite parking place on a hilltop out Cemetery Road, perhaps three miles from town. Even though I didn't have to go from "second base" (where I was now) to "home" on this one evening, I felt every minute without progress was lost opportunity.

My virginity had become an increasing, if still controlled embarrassment this spring. Because of my regular work habits, I did not date at school. A reputation for studiousness allowed me to evade the typical questions about sexual experience through my freshman year. Not an especially gifted student in high school, I knew I had to work hard to earn solid marks at the university. Methodical if not plodding, I succeeded by intense concentration and an addiction to precise procedure. Of course, I confirmed by silence the usual assumption that Linda and I did what other couples of long standing were thought to do.

But more and more as a sophomore I felt cut off from vital information, lost back in a childhood frame while my male contemporaries advanced into more challenging and more exciting arenas. That too might be expressed through an equation: E^1[xperience] + E^2 = K[nowledge of sexuality].

When I arrived back at Lost Spring, where the topographical map had told me a bench mark existed (1,234 feet above sea level), it was 2:10. I penciled the new elevation reading (1,255) in the log, set the needle back to 1,234, and spun the car around again to the south. I would calculate the elevation for that first well later. Right now, a hunch about the missing house was growing toward a certainty.

Again, I had learned enough things in a previous summer of well-finding to believe myself a pretty good detective. And ever since my state car had been parked on top of Walnut Ridge, my subconscious mind had been working. "Bingo!" I thought now: "Unrecorded changes." (I also calculated as I drove that the skies would remain clear in front of the present high pressure front--little change in pressure to affect the altimeter.)

As I passed the village's gas station/general store, one of the four standing buildings in this hamlet (there were also two churches and an abandoned grain warehouse), I caught a glimpse of a slim blonde girl in a light summer dress stepping into a black Ford pickup truck. She had probably just finished pumping gas. One long leg swinging up onto the floorboard made a picture in my mind I remember to this day: the rounded hip at a provocative angle pulling her dress up to show an inspiring flash of leg.

Such sightings occurred to me all summer in this job. I was gone from home through the week and spent much of that time fantasizing about parking with Linda and about potential "summer love" encounters I might stumble upon as I worked.

Even though I thought of myself as utterly committed to my "steady," I felt that, if, during the long summer weeks, I happened to find an attractive, innocent, backcountry girl who was willing to . . . well! I needn't tell my official girlfriend. If the myths about "the farmer's daughter" were true, I might solve the problem of my continuing virginity without Linda's assistance.

And this time my hunch about immanent sexual adventure was accurate.

Janet's Story III:
Genie in a Bottle

I had to break the bottle to get the papers out. I hated to do it, but there appeared to be no way to remove decades of mineral deposit from the glass. When I twisted the crusted cork with a pair of pliers, the bottle's neck cracked immediately. At least the papers inside were dry and perfectly legible.

This all happened in my father's basement shop in our home on the west side of Fairfield. We Masters lived in a remodeled old farmhouse at the beginning of a neighborhood known locally as "the Circle." Except for the half acre lot on which our two-story house stood, the rest of the original property had been broken down into a subdivision of two bedroom bungalows that helped provide homes for GI's returning from World War II.

I thumbed through the five sheets of fine stationary on which someone had written, in a beautiful hand, front and back. There was nothing to indicate immediately the time or place of the manuscript's composition or the name by which "a woman who lost an entire world" had been known.

I often took refuge in this shop, a place my father seldom went. He'd had it constructed when the original home, built in the last century, was modernized. But his medical practice generally kept him too busy for hobbies. He had the idea that he'd build or buy a weekend place at Lake of the Ozarks one day, but he'd never gone past looking over real estate brochures.

My mother always thought I should be refining my social skills in order to attract the wealthy and sophisticated young men she was sure were my ideal, so I often hid out in this shop. She had never seen Brad as completely adequate to her own dreams, and my rejection of this high school beau was something she could accept.

Before I broke open the bottle, I held it up in front of the light, trying to determine what, if anything, might be inside. I put an ear to it, as if I could hear its secrets the way you can hear an ocean's roar inside a conch shell. I rubbed its surface, wondering about the journey that had brought it to me.

What I wanted from this bottle, I suppose, was the famous genie who would grant me three wishes. Shoot, one wish would be enough! A new love interest, a fresh start at some different venture, a long-term goal to be achieved.

I giggled at the thought that the genie himself might be what I really wanted. He would materialize out of smoke, a man wrapped in a robe and wearing an exotic turban, completely unlike Brad Whitaker. This embodiment of ancient Eastern tradition would know a lot more about how to please a woman than my current lover!

I'd read the *Tales of the Arabian Nights*, of course, and sometimes imagined what it would be to like to encounter magic firsthand. So many characters in that work are faced with sudden transformations. Some are simple conversions: a faithful wife turns into a promiscuous woman; a husband is changed by jealousy. But others are fantastic: a man becomes a cow or sees a tree change into a demon.

Making love with Brad hadn't been like riding on a flying carpet, whisking me from the familiar to the foreign. In fact, it had been surprisingly unsurprising.

"I guess we have to set the date now," Brad had concluded afterwards. He leaned forward in the driver's seat, his hands resting on the steering wheel as if he were taking us someplace.

"Well, now," I'd hesitated. "There's time to think. This doesn't change anything."

"Doesn't change . . . ?" he wondered aloud.

Instead of the earth's moving or violins playing, the world had offered me no sign that I'd taken the right turn toward my destiny in the back seat of a Ford Galaxy. All I had by way of a vision, if it even was that, was a memory resurfacing--being at the spring. I might possibly have heard again the "plink" of the bottle breaking the surface of the water.

There could also have been some sort of rapid inventory in my mind of boys I'd met at school, boys who could have been potential romantic interests if I hadn't carried the idea of eventual marriage to Brad with me from home to college. Had there been someone I'd met on campus who represented a different future?

Of course, now I know that futures can come for women without men. I believe I had a destiny designed by the universe specifically for me. Derived from the deepest definition of my self, the path I was to follow had been shaped by the earth, by the non-human and the spiritual.

"Brad," I said. "We need to take a break from each other, I think. Let things cool down."

I knew this would be hard on him, adding to the disintegration my laugh had brought to his lovemaking. But I also sensed he would give in to my insistence, some chivalric notion of allowing the weaker sex time to accept the inevitable. I hoped in that delay to find some alternative to the path plotted for me by others.

There are those, of course, who would trace the beginning of my desire for something other than Brad further back, to incidents in my childhood. Freudians, according to my college psychology teacher, might point to the time when a neighborhood boy had shown me how to listen for railroad trains. There too I had put an ear to a cool surface, trying to connect with distant places.

Trains ran north of the Circle, through a cut behind the houses on Limestone Drive and along a flat stretch parallel to Black Street further east. There was a place all the kids knew about behind the Williamsons' where a path wound down to the tracks. I was probably seven or eight when a bunch of us slipped beyond the usual boundaries of neighborhood play.

"You have to put your ear right on the rail," said one boy, kneeling on the gravel beside the ties. "You can hear them way, way far away."

This was true, of course, the solid metal carrying the sound of wheels turning for many many more miles than air can.

"I'm not supposed to get dirty," I said, seeing grease and grime on the sides of the rail, even some spots on top. But the idea was mesmerizing, gaining contact with something far off in the distance. I saw several others getting down on their hands and knees.

Fairfield sits on a plateau in the Ozark foothills, and the Missouri Pacific Railroad tracks make a gradual, twenty-five mile climb east up from the Gasconade River valley. We could hear distant whistles a long time before freight trains loaded with Western cattle and oil labored into view. And that lonesome sound evoked other worlds--desert landscapes, frontier towns, mountain cabins.

"You won't get dirty," said another kid, though I could see that her own ear was smudged, her hands darkened. My mother would scold me more for a stain on my dress than for going somewhere I was not supposed to.

"Did you hear? Is a train coming?"

"Oh, yes. You'll hear."

All the others were trying it, so I knelt slowly and lowered an ear toward the cold metal.

"It won't work if you don't touch," said another of the boys. "Press your head down."

I looked at him and the others, then did as he said. My ear flattened to the metal, I listened and then heard a very faint humming or ringing, a high note sounded by tons of engine and freight bearing down on steel twenty miles away. Rrri-uunnngg. I was hypnotized.

When I tried to hear the bottle's secret more than a decade later, I recalled also the punishment I'd received when my mother discovered grease in my hair and black marks on my clothes: to bed right after dinner and no reading for a week. I hated lying there not ready to go to sleep.

Holding the manuscript pages in my hand at the workbench of my father's basement shop, I felt I would be able to do better with this than hear the sound of faraway travelers. Not just a tuneless hum, evocative though that train's sound had been. This was a powerful voice, speaking from another time, another place. I felt it was speaking to me.

Maybe there'd been a genie in the bottle after all!

Louis's Story III:
The Water Witch

What I remembered of the sexy girl at the Lost Spring's gas station was recorded on my brain in perhaps a second as I sped past. Looking at her, I was also recalling that I would have to find old man Carter and his well, take an elevation reading and mark the site on a map, then return to this location within sixty minutes to avoid my altimeter's drifting too far.

So even as I savored in my mind the erotic image of an unlearned backwoods siren, I knew it was almost certainly an illusion I would later find to be fading rapidly. This girl would turn out to be, if I ever saw her again, not nearly as pretty as I had imagined in that one fleeting moment. Nor certainly would she be as willing to entertain a traveling survey worker as I pretended.

Still, I was tempted to stop the '57 Chevy, circle back into town on some excuse (bench mark again?), and check out this phantom beauty in the Ford pickup. One reason for this brief hesitation had to be the simplicity of the girl's dress, which revealed an undisguised voluptuous form. Slender but fully developed, she was length and curves combined. No multilayered defense in place for this country girl, I bet!

But I slowed the car for only a moment before speeding back toward Green's Store and highway JJ. I had my work to do. If I kept moving, I would get in this one-hour run, and another, before the day was over. If Flowery Dress really lived around here, I'd have a chance to find her again.

On the way down Tom's Creek Road, my subconscious mind registered once again the remarkable natural beauty of the Ozarks. Before this week I had been working in counties near Kansas City, places already marked by suburban sprawl and commuter highways. Arkansas County was still as wild as the country found by early European settlers coming to the region.

Those emigrants learned about the territory from the native Osage peoples, who loved their land rich in furs and fruit. The mountain ridges still shaded fast-moving, clear streams, making crowding civilization seem remote or even irrelevant. The more I drove the county, linking images of the eye with markings on my map, the more I sensed I might one day learn to enjoy this lush countryside.

I was, and still am, a relentlessly visual person. I appreciate beauty, but I am almost entirely dependent on two-dimensional images for my understanding. My activities require visual guides, maps to the goals I seek.

To brush my teeth in the dormitory bathroom at that time, I needed a sink with a mirror. Somehow, watching the toothbrush work over the top left outside of teeth, behind the front teeth, the top right outside, and so forth, allowed me to do a thorough job. But if I were going by feel, I became convinced whole surfaces had been missed.

I also remember being terrible at a popular swimming pool game of my childhood, "Marco Polo." In this watery version of blind man's bluff, one person is "it" and tries to tag one of the other players. No player can get out of the pool, and "it" is required to keep his or her eyes closed.

"It" does have one privilege to his or her advantage: whenever "it" calls out "Marco," all the others must respond, "Polo." Judging direction by the sounds of "Polo," "it" swims toward a victim, who, if touched, becomes the next "it."

I could never tell which direction "Polo" was coming from, however, and tried to peek through slitted eyes to establish position. I suffered from a similar handicap in trying to follow my own fingers swimming through Linda's clothes.

Suddenly, I slammed on the brakes and jerked the wheels to the right, skidding to a stop on the edge of the gravel: there was a man standing right in the middle of the road.

"What the . . . ?" I said through clinched teeth. The car stopped short of the ditch, but just barely. The old man wandered up to the driver's window in a friendly manner, apparently not aware that he'd nearly caused an accident.

"Hello there, Sonny," he said, smiling.

"Hello." I decided it was still in my best interest to be polite. I was on Tom's Creek Road, after all, and this old timer might be able to help me find the Carter well. I climbed out of the car. "You live around here?"

"Could be. Let me see your hand."

"My hand?"

"Yes, your hand. I read palms."

"But I don't need my future told. I'm interested in the past. In the old Carter place." Still, perhaps as a reflex, something like shaking hands, I reached out and let the old man turn my hand palm upwards.

"The old Carter place? Um-hm. A long lifeline."

That's what they always say, I thought: we all want reassurance that death is far off into the future. We ought to ask whether the long life being predicted will be any good! "Wasn't this where Carter lived?"

"Could be." He looked more closely at my hand. "This says you're where you're supposed to be. What're you doing here?"

"That's just what I was trying to tell you. Looking for Carter. I need to find a well he had put down." I went through my customary spiel--the Survey; the drillers; the core samples--trying not to show irritation. "I know it's supposed to be on Tom's Creek Road. Isn't that where I am?"

"It's where you are. But not where you're heading. Who you need to see is Bobby."

"Bobby?" This old guy seemed to be diverting me farther and farther from the object of my search.

"Bobby Green's the witch around here."

Ah, I realized, the local dowser, the water witch, perhaps husband of old Mrs. Green back at the store.

I ran into this a lot in my work: the locals who believed certain men had the gift of finding water.

Holding a forked stick or metal rod by the ends of the "Y," the witch walked across land until the stem dipped, indicating water. A student of modern science, I didn't believe in such superstitions. But local residents routinely told me, if I wanted to find wells, "Bobby" was the person to talk to.

"Well, OK, if I run into Bobby," I offered, "I'll ask. But, say, *you* don't know where the Carter place is, do you?"

"Matter of fact, I do. It's down the lane there." He pointed to a gravel drive branching off Tom's Creek Road less than a hundred yards ahead, the one I had noted earlier going off on the wrong side of the road according to my map.

"Hm." I was speaking more to myself than to my companion. "I thought it would be on the right, not the left like Mrs. Green said."

"Mrs. Green?"

"At Green's Store, back on highway JJ."

"Oh, you mean Mrs. White. Those Greens been gone from there for thirty years. That's an old sign."

"Ah. Well, anyway, Mrs. *White* told me the lane was on the right, but my map . . . "

"Well now that road's been changed," my ancient guide interjected, pointing. "Used to run cross the creek down below there, up on the ridge over here." And then I understood: it *was* unrecorded changes.

The road had been redone since this map was drawn, probably to cross the creek in a more direct line. Early roads had followed the paths of walkers and horses. Over time--slowly in these parts-- engineers recharted even little county roads for automobile traffic. So the road I saw was not the one pictured on the map. It went on the other side of Carter place.

"Thanks, thanks a lot. I see where I need to go now." I reached out again to shake the old man's hand, still working to be polite. "Um, can I give you a lift?"

The old man smiled and nodded. "Why, yes. I'm going there myself."

So, shaking my head at this coincidence--why didn't he tell me that to begin with?--I cleared off the front seat and waited for my companion to ease himself in beside me.

Janet's Story IV: "Letter to an Unknown Friend"

"I don't know who will find these pages, if anyone, as I'm putting them inside a bottle, which I plan on throwing tomorrow into some rushing stream our wagon is crossing. There's nobody I could write to anyway, so I've decided I might as well trust Providence to deliver this sad tale."

"We'll be on the way East then, our remaining worldly belongings fit into a worn out wagon we hope will make it as far as St. Louis and the railroad station. While we've been packing--and discarding-- these last weeks, I've been reviewing the decline of our affairs. And now I see what dark force caused our misfortune. That doom, it turns out, is as old as the Johns family itself, its Fabulous Fountain."

"Let me start with who I am: Lucy Rivers Johns, granddaughter of the more well-known Luther Taylor Johns, who founded an iron works west of St. Louis fifty years ago, in about 1826. Granddaddy was a poor farmer back in Tennessee early in the century, and he decided to try his luck out on the frontier. West of the Mississippi, he found Indian guides who showed him where to fish, where to hunt. He showed them his invention, which always amazed folks and made them his friends."

"Luther Johns had never known who his daddy was. He came to awareness of the world, I guess you might say, as an orphan begging and stealing in and around Richmond, Virginia. But he had a knack for making things, and he learned from blacksmiths, carpenters, tinkers, anyone he spent time with."

"Eventually, he got to farming land no one else wanted, using his own system of irrigation. He married and had a son. But, what with hard times and blight and a few bad investments, he found himself just a step ahead of starvation and ruin."

"Cold Spring Iron Works finally made him famous and made his family rich. But his descendants are being forced to abandon everything he created for an uncertain future, me most of all."

"I don't mind getting out of the iron business, which had pretty much run its course anyway. But leaving the place I care for is more than I can tolerate. Sometimes I think I'll throw myself instead of the bottle into the river and end it all drowned in the waters of my beloved homeland."

"You see, all the time I was growing up, I believed the Johns family would live forever in this beautiful country, the only place I've ever known. Our house wasn't exceptional, but the land around it was to me just like the Garden of Eden."

"Granddaddy, as I said, always had a way with tools. He could build anything, from a house to a smelting furnace to a sawmill to his special device that would pump water uphill--his Fabulous Fountain."

"That talent flourished out here on the frontier, and his son and his family (Momma and me) were rich enough we didn't have to do anything but manage the business after he passed on. Momma turned our property into a paradise. She put in flower gardens and fish ponds and pathways through the forest. I lived in a fairyland until things fell apart. My favorite place, of course, was the spring, nestled into the hillside down below the house."

"Cold Spring, we call it, a translation of the Indian name, I'm told. The water's so cold you'd think it would be ice. It flows off down the valley as a stream that doesn't have a name, so far as I knew. They say it goes on down to the faraway Gasconade, but I never knew anyone who actually followed it to the river.

"That's the thing about this country--so many Spring and streams and rivers, many linked deep underground, you can't see the whole thing in its entirety or what's connected to what or how. I do know that, you drop something in the water here, it could end up anywhere, years later."

"Whenever I went down to the spring--and I did that a lot--I would think about where the water would go, what sort of journey it followed. (I never thought I'd have to take a long journey myself!) In that spot I feel connected to deep, old things. It's quiet, mostly just the birds and forest creatures moving softly about. Maybe the wind shifting the trees higher up the hill, but the spring itself is sheltered. This is Mother Earth to me, and Cold Spring's steady bubbling the ancient voice of Father Time. Beginnings are here, origins, a heart of the country."

"But come dawn, Cold Spring will be in the past. I suspect I'll never stand there again."

"Building up the family business, you see, was a happy story, one we all loved to tell. But Luther's son, my Daddy, has succeeded in turning that same enterprise into a tale of woe. Martin Johns is better at spending than making, and he doesn't have that special genius of his daddy, turning out the thing that's needed at just the right moment."

"What led Luther Johns to money, as I said, also brought about his family's collapse, the journey we start tomorrow. His arrival in this country, half a century ago, was made easy by two factors: genius and simple good fortune."

"You see, those Indian guides who showed Luther this land wore paint on their faces and bodies with a distinctive reddish-orange tint to it, something he hadn't seen on any other Indians. He didn't think it came from berry or bark or leaf. And he was right: it came from the ground. Those Indians--Osage they were--eventually led him to a rich iron ore deposit near Cold Creek."

"Luther understood that coming settlers would need metal for equipment and repair. The stream gave him power and a way of washing the ore and flushing the tailings. So he built wooden sluices and made his own bricks and figured out what wood to burn to get his furnace up to the required heat. In five years he was mining and smelting and selling all the iron he could."

"The problem was, no one was thinking way off into the future, the day when everything would run out. Nor the time when somebody would develop a better system even then Luther Taylor Johns'. While Luther had continued to improve the iron works as long as he lived, my Daddy spent the profits in crazy investment schemes--distant gold mines that never paid out, inflated commercial concerns, the patent medicines of accomplished quacks."

"The War gave us one last boost of business, producing material for guns and railroads. But less than a decade after that, while Daddy was scouring the papers for more ways to throw away our money, the ore about played out. Too, we'd cut down so many trees, we couldn't keep the furnaces going without paying more than we were bringing in for lumber from further west."

"And then, just about three years ago, improved railroads began to deliver better products from Pittsburgh at cheaper prices than we could offer. Those businessmen and engineers back East had gone way past the frontier system Luther had developed and which my father never had the vision to refine. Once the slide started, we went to bankruptcy in a rush. Of course, we'd been building up debt for a good while too."

"I think now of my Granddaddy following old hunting trails west from St. Louis in the 1820s. He won the help of Indians by showing them one ingenious device he'd made on his own, his Fountain. Good fortune and his genius created a special world."

"Of course, human ingenuity was older than he was, and it broke out again back East. In the beginning Luther had his Fabulous Fountain, but by 1870 they had richer ore, hotter furnaces, and faster delivery systems. Damn the railroads! My Daddy borrowed and sold and gambled. So Momma and I get in a wagon tomorrow with all our worldly possessions to what end we don't know. At the same time, strangers from the bank will take over our house and all the land we once owned, including Cold Spring itself. I never earned this richness, but I'm losing it now. Naturally, it was all to come to me one day."

"I never knew it until this night, but I realize now I'd have liked to preserve this beautiful place, Cold Spring, keep it as simple and rich as God made it so others could enjoy what I've known. So, I'll seal up these pages in my bottle, which I'll tuck among my bags that go on the wagon. Somewhere short of St. Louis, they'll enter one of the territory's mighty rivers and begin a journey I can't see the end of. God grant they find a kind hand, someone who might want to take an interest in this sad story of my Cold Spring."

(signed) "A woman who lost an entire world."

Louis's Story IV: Bobby Green

With my passenger beside me, I pulled up a rise to an old white frame farmhouse with sheer curtains lazily swaying in the open windows. There was perhaps a half-acre of yard, nicely mowed, a few flower beds with red and orange blossoms resting in the sun, an orderly vegetable garden to the side.

Once again I silently congratulated myself on my manner with the simple folk who lived in Missouri's backwoods. I had learned how to be courteous, and I was always careful to dress in an unthreatening manner. A suit suggested the government ("revenuer"), but blue jeans and T-shirt would not be taken seriously. So I'd settled in time on khakis, a white dress shirt and tie but no jacket, plain black shoes (when the occasion called for it, I had to set out across fields or through woods).

The appearance I presented to small-town residents and farmers, though, almost always disguised the full distance I couldn't help feeling from their rural lifestyle. My goal was to use my education to rise to the top of a commercial or government organization. I would hold meetings in a sprawling complex in the suburbs of St. Louis. Field work was only preparation, brief, I hoped, for an office career.

In fact, the true goal of my finding this summer was not wells spread across the state of Missouri, but another solid entry on my resume. I didn't plan to carry knowledge of geology or irrigation or plumbing with me to a higher level of the Survey's operations. The idea was eventually to manage others who did the actual work of gathering and sorting.

Well, what do you know! There was Flowery Dress standing beside her Ford pickup in the turnaround beside the barn! I had a hunch I'd see her again. Fortuitous indeed!

"Hello, Roberta," said my companion, pulling himself up from the car seat on the car door. "You're early."

"I finished up in town ahead of time, Mr. Carter," she said, smiling as at an old friend.

"Carter?" I wondered. Was this *the* Carter? Shoot!

Pointing at me, he said, "This here's--um, don't believe I caught the name--Mr. . . . ?"

"Clark. I'm with the Missouri Geological Survey. A well-finder, come to look for a well put down here, uh, sometime about the first World War. Maybe 1915." I studied my passenger. "This is *your* place? *You're* Carter?"

"Sure. I've lived here since '88. But I don't remember exactly where your well is. I was gone when they put it in. In France. We had a well that was dug by hand, but it gave out. They replaced it while I was away, but didn't go deep enough. We went to carrying water up from the spring, like we'd done before. We didn't get a good well until after the Second World War."

"OK. I think we have that second one. I see the well house out there in the field." I checked the information printed on the Survey slip and pointed to the small white building several hundred feet from the house. "What I need to know is where that old one was put down. Do you think it was at the same place?"

"Well now, I can't exactly recall, probably not. They filled that dry one in, I believe, when it gave out. I never minded getting water from the spring, though, myself. This lady's daddy put in electricity a few years back, I don't know why. The old oil lamps and wood stove was all I needed."

"My dad's his nephew," explained Roberta, though what relation that made her to Mr. Carter was beyond me. And I wasn't interested in the extra family history he was wandering through. My single objective was the well's location, not some convoluted story about people and events. I was a finder, and once I'd reached by goal, the many steps leading up to that point could be forgotten.

"OK, but the well . . . ?"

"Roberta here can find that for you, if it's anywhere about."

"Oh?" I smiled now at this young woman who, in fact, was as beautiful as I'd imagined when I saw her earlier. About my age, open features, a twinkle in her eye. Talk about a finder's keeper!

"Yep," continued Carter. "There's supposed to be a metal pipe in the ground where that well was. Should be big enough to find, four or five inches across. But I never seen it in all my years. Could be buried pretty deep. Could be it got lost."

"Ah-ha, metal detector. Is that how you'd find it?"

The Survey used these devices on certain occasions, and I'd learned how they work at school. They emit radio waves, which bounce off different substances in characteristic manners, a kind of radar. Sweeping over an area's surface, you'll get pinging where metal is buried. You can't tell what metal might be there, but you can come pretty close to pinpointing its location. It was an instrument I appreciated, though it wouldn't have been sensible to use in my work.

"No, no metal detectors," she laughed. "I'm the water witch. I'll dowse for it." She walked over to her pickup and, rummaging around behind the seat, came out with a forked metal rod, the shape of the letter "Y." It made me think of a mandrake root, the plant which tradition says resembles a man's body and legs.

"I, uh, I guess that would be OK." Then I thought to myself: I get it: Bobby = Roberta. The water witch Carter had told me about was Roberta (Bobby) Green, a young woman not an old man. I was sure having a hard time getting the facts straight in this case!

I was willing to accept Bobby's help, but I knew I'd have to find more confirmation than her "witching" to place this well. Mr. Mitchell, the man I reported to, would make me the butt of coffee hour jokes if I claimed to have located the well by dowsing.

"Maybe there's someone we can ask, another family member . . . ?" I said, turning to Mr. Carter as

Bobby started across the yard. She was covering the area in a systematic fashion, holding her simple device horizontally out in front of her.

"No," said Carter. There's nobody left but me who was around back then. I've been back here since '17. Now, of course, there's been people to come for a spell . . . ."

As Mr. Carter began a rambling account of the many visitors who had stayed at his farm over the years, and as Bobby swept back and forth in front of us, humming softly to herself, I felt a sudden, deep fatigue coming on. It had happened to me more than once on long days of well-finding in the summer heat.

This particular search now seemed endless, a series of turnings onto smaller and smaller roadways. I had begun on a stretch of four-lane highway, taken a major north-south United States highway through smaller and smaller towns to this out-of-the way locality. Then I was on a winding state road, a narrow county blacktop, a dirt road, a driveway. My mind drifted back once more to my frustrating Saturday night date with Linda.

I'd brought "Smoky Joe" to rest ten yards down a lane between two corn fields. I turned to Linda and found her ready to neck after four hours of close dancing. (Neither of us had learned the newer dances that succeeded the Twist, preferring the 1940s style of our parents.)

Linda had the appropriate dress for the semiformal occasion--and, I suspected, all the recommended undergarments. While her shoulders were bare now (the sweater she'd carried was folded neatly on the seat beside her), the rest of her was predictably encased in a veritable armor: dress, corset, slip, garter belt, brassier, panties, and perhaps more. I suggested we move to the back seat and was surprised when she agreed.

I was astounded when my deliberate reaching inspired no objection. Then I realized her armor was effective on its own. I could get under dress and slip, below corset, around garter belt, away from brassier, and to panties. But all this together made such a tight package the site I felt for at its center was invulnerable, unless she were willing to discard everything. And then it was 11:45; time was up.

Bobby the water-witch in her simple dress strolled by me one more time. Carter the ancient native wandered through years of memory. A strange new thought began to take shape in my tired brain.

Janet's Story V: Decision

I was struck by these particular words about Cold Spring written by Lucy Rivers Johns: "This is Mother Earth to me, and Cold Spring's steady bubbling the ancient voice of Father Time. Beginnings are here, origins, a heart of the country." Where was I, Janet Masters, in relation to a beginning, a heart of life's meaning? What journey from that origin was I on? Toward what end was I moving, slowly or in a rush? I realized I didn't have any idea. I decided to go to my spring to seek an answer.

A trip to the spring would have to wait, of course, until after work the next day. When I'd read the message in the bottle, it was nearly my bedtime and certainly too late for a cross-country hike in the dark. But I'm sure you can see already that I'd connected my spring to the one Lucy talked about.

She wrote that she was throwing the bottle into a stream on the way to St. Louis, after leaving Cold Spring. The place I visited had no name, that I knew of. It was just where Fairfield kids had hiked to and sat around for generations--"the spring." That bottle could have gone downstream, washed into an underground river, resurfaced magically in the very place Lucy had loved.

I remembered talking to this guy one time in Columbia, a student at Mizzou. We were at some Stephens dormitory mixer. As I recall, both of us had steadies back home, so we weren't looking for dates, just enjoying the music and the dancing, a break from studying. He knew a lot about Missouri's rock and water.

"We're a honeycomb," he said. "Missouri doesn't have any natural lakes, but we're where two of the nation's great rivers join. And tributaries of the Mississippi and the Missouri are coming in from every county."

"Yeah?" I was mostly being polite, not terribly interested at this point. But some of what he said stuck with me and came back months later when I thought about Lucy's bottle's journey.

"You can't dig down into the earth anywhere in the state without finding, eventually, good, clean water. It's really like we're floating on a series of underground lakes, all connected like the Great Lakes. The land we walk on is actually islands separated by all our rivers and streams and ponds and creeks."

"I hadn't ever thought about it like that."

"Well, when you do think about it, consider the sink holes up where the Missouri and the Mississippi come together."

"Sink holes?"

"Great craters where bedrock has been eroded underneath and the land falls in. The gravel roads that wander into that area are built on the rims of the sinks because the ground inside is so soft, where all the rainfall gathers and disappears. You don't want to fall through to some underground ocean."

"I see."

"It makes you realize, we're up here on dirt and rock islands kind of drifting atop the world's water, little ships journeying who knows where."

"How do you know all this?"

I assumed that he was a geology major. But just then the band started up a loud number and we drifted apart as kids do at such events and I never learned any more about him. But his mini-lecture on Missouri's topography stayed with me, surfacing like my very bottle to offer an explanation of its journey.

To get a real answer, I figured I'd have to do some research. But, hey, research was what I enjoyed as a student, wasn't it? I had recently reminded Brad that I was a potential high school history teacher. So I decided to take my lunch break the next day at our public library and see what I could find out about the Cold Spring Iron Works and the Johns family. It turned out that I got some background information from my favorite office visitor even before I consulted any books at the library.

My customarily boring long morning as receptionist had been moving more swiftly than usual as I reviewed in my mind Lucy John's story. She filled in the gaps and silences around patients arriving and sitting and leaving. The "lost world" she had referred to might not be as lost as she feared. While much of the area right around Fairfield had been cleared and farmed at different times over the last century, we still had patches of virgin forest where Ozark ridges were too steep to cultivate and paved roads had never penetrated. Rivers and streams cut up the landscape, isolating many hard-to-reach corners. If I could locate an account of the iron works' founding, I might well be able to identify its location.

Thinking about all this must have inspired the unfocused look on my face Mrs. Sophie Anderson noted when she came in, although she assumed another cause. "Dreaming about a long lost lover, my dear?" she asked brightly, leaning on her cane.

"Oh! Hi, Mrs. Anderson. No . . . no, I . . . Just daydreaming. Did you have an appointment?"

"Not with your father, Janet. But now I do want to see him. You've found some romantic interest since I was in here earlier this week, and he ought to know about it."

"That's not so, but I do have an interest. And you might be able to help me with it. You've lived in Fairfield for so long, and you know everybody. Do you know anything about the Johns family and the Cold Spring Iron Works?"

"Sure, it was Lucy Johns' grandfather that started the operation. Failed after the Civil War, I think."

"You didn't know Lucy Johns, Lucy Rivers Johns, did you?"

"Lucy? No. Well, not really." Mrs. Anderson hesitated, then continued. "But I did know of her. Around the time of the first World War, I guess, she used to come here from somewhere back East. The family owned land west of town, as I recall. Maybe she did. Anyway, she was a bit strange, 'eccentric,' I think you might say. And I . . . I kept my distance."

An uneasy grin suggested she knew that she was considered more than a little "eccentric" herself. She had, for instance, a house full of animals that she bred for laboratory research.

"But she grew up here?"

"Grew up on land near the Iron Works, I was told. I don't know exactly where that was. Probably the same place she used to visit when she came back, once with her little baby girl. She had money, I do remember that. I think she'd married some Wall Street financier, a banker. But when she came back to Phipps County, she was mostly alone. Why do you want to know, Janet?"

"Well, I was . . . um . . . just doing some reading about county history, and I came across her name." For some reason I wanted to keep my bottle and its letter secret, at least for right now. I didn't think it valuable or anything, just private. And now I was getting some great clues about what had happened after Lucy left Missouri--marriage and returning to the region.

"We have had some odd characters around Fairfield over the years," Mrs. Anderson continued. "We're a bit out of the way, you know. Even though a lot of people pass through here on Route 66, they're generally headed somewhere else. California usually. Folks that stop here, especially those that go off into the woods like Lucy Johns did, they don't want much to do with society. And what their long histories might be we never learn."

"I see."

"You go five miles from the highway, you know, down some dirt road or another, you might as well be all the way to Arkansas County much as the world's likely to find you."

"I guess you're right."

"Now me, I never wanted to be cut off from mankind, even if I've outlived all of my own family, or they've gone elsewhere."

Mrs. Anderson had had two sons, one in Atlanta and one in Philadelphia, who had always tried to get her to come live with them. But she'd wouldn't leave her own home and pursuits.

"Besides," she concluded with another wink and a look around the waiting room. "I haven't given up on finding another man."

That made me chuckle, of course. And it turned into one of those deep, satisfying laughs that start gently but build and continue. I realized I had a new mission in life: to find out more about Lucy Rivers Johns and Cold Spring. After that, I didn't know what I'd do, but, for some reason, I felt confident that the path I should follow would appear before me. I would begin by following the letter in the bottle back to its source.

Louis's Story V: Source

As old man Carter rambled on in reminiscence and young Roberta Green strode across the Arkansas County farmyard, my mind wandered ahead in time to count all the wells I would have to find this summer in earning the money for fall tuition. Then I saw the courses I would take this year (advanced physics, calculus II, managerial economics) just to get to the specific classes in my engineering major, and then all the specialized courses needed to qualify me for entry into this profession (hydrogeology, thermodynamics and statistical mechanics, topology).

Then I envisioned the mind-numbing routine jobs I would endure before reaching my goal of a comfortable supervisory position, the office job cushioned from competition and review. At the same time, I knew it would be necessary to persist just as relentlessly in building a family life to support me on the way to and after retirement. That meant finding someone to be mother of my children, loyal spouse, faithful housekeeper, nurse and sometime counselor. I would have to join Rotary, coach little league baseball, take a turn as poll watcher. It was a daunting operation.

Then the financial structure that would have to be put in place piece by piece to sustain a role in society: insurance plans, good mortgage on property with solid resale value, reliable automobile (maybe

61

two), varied retirement investments such as tax-free bonds and more risky stock options. It was staggering.

Again I watched the country girl cross the yard, heard Carter nostalgically recalling the time rats got in the potato cellar, the years of high water, deaths of farm animals.

I saw the survey car parked in the drive and realized the front left tire was flat. Shoot!

Without even thinking, I knew also that my time on this particular well-finding run had run out: the altimeter would have drifted too far for me to calculate readings accurately, even if Bobby Green or I were to find the old well site.

Then another thought struck me: how many things had I gotten confused in this case? *Green*'s Store is run by Mrs. *White*; the Carters' place is *south* not *north* of Tom's Creek Road; *Green* the water-witch is not an *old codger* but *a beautiful young woman*, Roberta not Robert; the figure in the road is not some lost senile old man but Carter, the owner of the well I am seeking, a World War I veteran who seems to have survived on his own for decades in one of the most remote parts of the whole country.

Bobby meanwhile swept up, pausing just a few feet in front of me.

"Here's what you're looking for," she said, pointing near her feet with the Y-shaped wand held in both hands.

"Hmm?" Looking down, I saw nothing but the little tufts of grass making up Mr. Carter's lawn.

Then, in order to bend down and show me what she'd found, Bobby gathered the hem of her flowery dress in one hand. Squatting, she balanced on her heels, and I nearly blacked out as a long reach of tanned legs was exposed. I felt I should look away, but couldn't. Could it be that she is wearing no underwear! Could it be I am seeing . . . ?

I followed the line of her finger's pointing and inspected more closely the grass in front of her knees. And then I realized, of course, that Bobby was not revealing herself, only giving me a clear view of the ground. Oh, what hormones and tiredness and frustration will do to a twenty-year-old male!

I dropped to my knees then, weakened by the heat, worn from the day's events, weary from my own longing.

"Right here," said Bobby Green, pointing with her slender fingers to one small spot.

I looked. "There's nothing here but dirt and grass." I put a hand down, patting all around. "Nothing."

But one place felt a bit soft, spongy. I pushed on the spot of yard with a couple of fingers, and the dirt sagged. I poked a finger into the ground, pulling a plug perhaps three inches in diameter loose from the top end of a buried metal pipe. Tearing out the little bit of sod and brushing the opening clear, I leaned forward and stared down into a dark hole. For all I knew, it went to the very center of the earth!

"You've found it," I admitted. "The well."

"Not bad for a country girl," she said with the slightest mocking sound in her voice. Looking up, however, I saw a pleasant smile on her face.

"Yes, . . . er . . . I mean, of course, you've found it. And . . . and thank you. Let's see, I need to get my altimeter. And I'll just mark this on the map." I stood and gazed around the yard, trying to judge the distance from the house, my relationship to the road. As dizzy as I was from the day's events, though, I suspect I looked as if I couldn't find the car I'd driven here in.

Bobby and her--what? uncle? great uncle? uncle twice removed?--walked over to the porch. She was still carrying her dowser's stick.

I decided to take an altimeter reading even though it couldn't be reliable. Since I already had an elevation for the newer well out there at the well house, and it wouldn't be five feet different from this, I could cheat just a little bit in eyeballing a reading. I could count this well as found. What I couldn't do, though, was claim a solid sense of my own location.

This wild goose chase for an old well had made me wonder what I was doing with myself, with this plan for a bureaucratic career. I was endorsing all the tools and learning and structure of the future but without genuine conviction. In truth, I wanted something much simpler, more basic, down to earth (if you'll forgive this pun from a well-finder).

The parallel lines and concentric circles on the topographic map where I pinpointed Carter's well might have represented for me the confusing conventions of 1950s-style courting. The web of geographic coordinates were like the elaborate privileges and prohibitions of dating--calling on the phone, paying for the movies, making small talk about fashion, current events, pop music. Underneath all of that were the things that mattered, like rock, soil, water, trees. How *did* you get to the truth, ground level? How *did* you find a place where you connected to elemental forces, to the universal human condition?

Bobby seemed to possess and to stand for the goals I desired, and not simply as an object of lust. She spoke and moved in concert with Mr. Carter and the farmland where he'd lived out a full life. Her dowser's rod linked her to the hidden riches of the earth. And her eyes sparkled with pleasure at her surroundings. I, on the other hand, was struggling to use all of this only for my own selfish ends.

I wanted a father as I had so many times in my adolescent years, someone to offer a record of his own experiences and some clues to guide me along a parallel path. What should I do?

"Where're you staying while you hunt wells?" Bobby's question woke me from my reveries. Carter was standing on his porch watching her go. She had walked out to where I was gathering my equipment.

"Oh! Um, back in Arkansas, the Ozark Motel." This was the county seat, twenty-five miles north and east. Well-finders spent the week on the road, returning to Survey headquarters in Fairfield each Friday to turn in their finds.

"I'll be over there day after tomorrow, doing some shopping. Maybe I'll see you?" She was backing up toward her truck, giving me a parting wave and a sweet smile.

"We could . . . um . . . get a burger together?" I offered, surprised at myself. This was completely impulse, something uncharacteristic for me, the planner and plotter.

"I'll see if you're at your motel Wednesday 'bout six." She jumped into her truck and pulled the door smartly shut.

Whoa! Perhaps I'd had it wrong. I'd assumed this young lady was completely in control of her life, already having everything she needed. But this looked like she was seeking me out.

"Great. I'll be there."

And I was there, but, as happened with so many other things in this week of well-finding, I learned that her interest in me came from causes I never suspected. Even so, I've never regretted what happened that summer night so many years ago.

Janet's Story VI:
Rock Wall

I hoped to get inspiration about my bottle at the spring when I went there after work the next day. The ghost of Lucy Rivers Johns might appear, I speculated, ready to tell her life story and thus give direction to my own.

But, before I ever got to the spring, work, for a change, provided some excitement. A boy my age came in with a bloody rag on his forehead.

"Is this Dr. Masters'?" he asked, gazing around the room with the eye not covered by the rag.

"Yes. But you'd better sit down. Let me call the nurse."

The boy looked familiar, but I couldn't place him immediately. He might have been someone I went to school with in earlier grades. Or perhaps he'd gone to our church at one time.

After a quick examination there in the waiting room, Nurse Riley declared, "This looks worse than it is. You've split the skin just above the eyebrow. There's a lot of blood, but the doctor will stitch you up. You'll be back doing what you were doing in half an hour."

"I'm working at Stony Court," he explained, nodding toward the north. The Stony Court Motel was across Kingshighway (Business Route 66) and up about a block from my father's office.

"Um . . . what's your name?" I asked. "Are you a regular patient here?"

"I'm Freddy Sill. You know me."

"Right! Sure," I said, turning to the files to look for a chart, though I still couldn't place this boy. He must have come into the office before, but I didn't remember him.

"You look up his record," said Mrs. Riley, directing the boy down the hall with a hand under his arm. "And I'll get him cleaned up and ready for Dr. Masters. Second door on the left."

"How did you . . . how did that happen?" I asked, gesturing toward the top of his head as he turned to go.

"Stupid Mr. Bachmann hurrying us on the rock. We told him to leave us to do the job right."

Stony Court, where this rock was, had been a favorite stopping point of cross country travelers for many years. Right now the facing of the motel was being changed, Ozark stone replaced with a more modern asbestos siding. So I assumed some accident during that process had bloodied young Freddy Sill.

Sill, Sill? I didn't see a chart for Freddy Sill (Simms, Simpson, Stillman, but no Fred, Freddy, or Frederick Sill). And I could not recall a previous visit.

Stony Court began to lose business after the Route 66 four-lane bypass was built north of Fairfield, about half a dozen years ago. Local businessmen generally believed, according to my father, that there were only two ways for roadside establishments like Stony Court to respond to traffic's being redirected away from them: relocate to a place visible from the new four-lane Route 66, or increase highway advertising enough to draw travelers into town. Mr. Bachmann's approach included more advertising and the idea of improved service.

We talked about such concerns in the office when things were slow, as Fairfield's prosperity is directly related to Route 66. The town sells to travelers, but we also benefit now (and will moreso in the future) from a central position on this major artery moving goods east and west from the nation's midsection.

Stony Court's owner, Mr. Bachmann, had recently decided to remodel the motel, adding the latest conveniences--Cold Cavern Air-conditioning, Deeper Sleeper Mattresses, and color television.

The major networks had announced about this time that all their programming would soon be in color, though Fairfield's distance from major stations (Jefferson City, Springfield, St. Louis) made reception for us problematic. Most home sets here were still black and white. But Bachmann figured travelers from large cities would be used to color. So he gambled on improvements in transmission and reception.

In addition to the amenities Bachmann planned to feature on existing billboards, he was posting pictures to show the motel's new look. Stony Court had been a fine example of "Ozark Giraffe," a variation on older buildings made with cobblestone walls. In these Missouri houses, many built in the

1930s, thin, irregularly shaped pieces of local limestone, each approximately a foot square, are set in cement. It's not a rock wall through and through, but it's certainly stable and requires no upkeep.

Ozark Giraffe produces an inexpensive veneer that also fits in well, I've always thought, with the natural landscape. Our rivers and creeks cut into the hills, showing high bluffs of limestone. It's perhaps the most characteristic view from Missouri's Route 66, as, once you leave St. Louis, you're mostly passing through countryside. So the vertical face of odd shaped rocks on Stony Court resembles what you see from the surface of our many rivers--the Gasconade, the Osage, the Missouri.

I have learned a lot over the years about the art of Ozark Giraffe, a folk craft passed on and refined from generation to generation. And it would become a key element in the emerging identity of Route 66 Spring. But right now all I knew was that it was going out at Stony Court so that something new could come in.

I thought, by the way, that Bachmann should change the name of his motel, as it wasn't going to look like a "Stony Court" any longer. Apparently the misnomer didn't bother him. Nor, I suspect, did the occasional injury to workers like Freddy Sill cause him to worry about the cost of such alterations. Bachmann had a reputation of being willing to cut corners when it was to his advantage, though the motel he ran was a nice one.

"Good as new!" announces the young man who works for Bachmann thirty minutes after Mrs. Riley had escorted him away from the waiting room. He's standing in front of my desk, sporting a grin and a large Band-Aid over his left eye. I know there are stitches.

"Good! Ah, I don't seem to be able to find a file. Are you sure you're one of Dr. Master's patients?"

"No, no, I've never come here before.

"I thought you said . . . oh, never mind. Here fill out this form." I should have done this when he first came in.

He sits down in a nearby chair, but looks up over the clipboard I've given him. "I just said you know me, not that I'm a patient of your father's."

It does seem I'm supposed to know who he is, as he understands I'm the doctor's daughter. This is embarrassing, but I can't call up a thing from memory. Maybe I met him at college?

In another minute he hands me back the form and says, "The little house near yours on Black Street?"

I look at the form and try to tie it to what he's saying. "That's where you live?"

"That's where I used to live once, when we were both kids. It was only a few months, with my aunt and uncle, the Potters."

"Ah." I knew the house, at Black Street and Valley Lane, a short block from our house on Hill Street. "Yes, I know them."

And then a memory did come back of another child my age, years ago. He was staying with relatives while his family built a house somewhere. I couldn't recall the exact details or draw up a clear picture of a face. I looked more closely at this young man, trying to imagine him a child.

"We used to play together, us and a bunch of neighborhood kids. There were kids all over that place!"

"Oh, yes, the Circle." We were a babyboomer neighborhood, dozens of children born after the troops came home from World War II. Black Street was the road in to the Circle from Highway 00.

"I remember getting you to come down to the railroad tracks. They run behind the houses on . . . what was that other street?"

"Limestone."

"OK. So, anyway, we'd put our ear down on the railroad track to see if we could tell if a train was coming. You could hear them twenty miles away. That was great, like some great secret was coming into your life from far, far away. But you got in trouble with your mama for doing it, didn't you?"

"I did. But I didn't stop doing it!"

"Maybe if you'd listened closely today," he said, turning to leave. "You'd have heard me coming back into your life!"

Louis's Story VI: Timing

For all my fantasizing about a hot summer romance, I could construct no scenario that ended with Bobby Green and me in bed at the Ozark Motel in Arkansas, Missouri. I'm pretty sure now it wasn't because I was haunted by guilt about possibly betraying my relationship to Linda Forrester.

I had been imagining erotic entanglings inside a motel room all summer, just me and some well endowed country girl I'd predicted living in the house just around the bend, over that hill, on the next farm. All of them ended in the obligatory cigarette smoked with our heads on pillows, a sheet pulled up over spent, naked bodies. Linda didn't figure in these scenarios.

But this water-witch of surprising beauty seemed to possess so much calm self-assurance that I foresaw my doing what she wanted, rather than the other way around. And this was unsettling because I doubted if she wanted a no-commitment tumble with an itinerant state Geological Survey employee.

I had been a meticulous arranger of situations since . . . well, since, I guess, my father's passing. But how I might get my way with Bobby failed to come to me as a vision while I pursued and located wells the next two days.

I was nine years old when that happened--my father's death. I was young enough to be completely vulnerable but old enough to feel the reach of loss for me and my mother.

Dad was one of three successful jewelers in Fairfield. He had a store on Fairfield Street, having taken over the business of the elderly man he'd worked with since he was in high school during the Depression.

Quixote's (the name stayed when my father took over) had been in existence since the early 1900s. A cautious approach to inventory--only established brands of traditional goods--had enabled the store to survive the ups and downs of the regular business cycle, though it never made anyone rich. My father followed the pattern created by his mentor, Mr. Perez, to modest financial comfort. But he did have an occupational weakness.

Samuel Clark loved mechanical timepieces-- weight driven grandfather and coo coo clocks, spring activated pocket and wrist watches, ancient hourglasses and sundials. In the most vivid recollection I have of my father, he is perched on a stool, the jeweler's eyeglass held in place by a one-eyed squint. A smile spreads across his face as he works on some gear, a balance wheel, the turning rods and wheels of tiny machinery. He loved intricacy and precision.

The shop he worked in was itself tiny, perhaps eight feet of open space between two rows of glass cabinets. There was so little space behind those cabinets that my parents had to lean over sideways to pull aside sliding doors and bring things up for a customer's inspection.

My dad's work space, no more than six by ten feet, was behind a back counter, where the cash register sat on one side and a passageway made a gap on the other side. A piece of the counter lifted up on hinges for employees to come out from the back. His work bench was on one wall, a supply closet on the other next to a tiny bathroom. All his stock was displayed in glass cases, which opened from the back, or stored in drawers beneath the cases that opened into the center of the store.

Still, in that crammed space was a wonderful variety. Besides timepieces, he carried jewelry (necklaces, earrings, bracelets, cuff links, tie pins), writing implements (fountain pens, mechanical pencils, calligraphy sets), and decorative items (paper weights, fancy ash trays, elegant little bowls to hold candy or nuts).

Most fascinating to me were the clocks mounted all over the store--on the walls above the display cases, all around Dad's work space, over the door and two plate-glass windows, even a small number hung from the ceiling. They were his prize collection, and only a few were ever offered for sale.

Since he never had much capital, he bought supposedly defunct old clocks at auctions, through second hand stores, or from individuals who came by the store hoping to unload some family heirloom for a little money. He then restored them with painstaking care.

There was a feature of his clock collection that, for many years, I viewed as a product of his own character flaw, a flaw I unfairly linked to his early demise.

While every clock visible in his shop worked, they didn't all work together. That is, some ran a bit fast, others slow, and a few irregularly, speeding up gradually or slowing down for no reason he could ever fully divine.

Built in different eras (from the fifteenth century to the middle of the twentieth), with varied materials (wood, metal, even bone), and by many hands, each had a distinctive character, a unique tick-tock of verger checked by pallets. It's a matter of the movement's driving force and its restraint, the work's train and its escapement. No two handmade clocks are the same.

"Look at this chain and drum, Louis," he'd tell me, pointing to a Victorian clock pulled free from its dark marble case. "You'd think the chain too weak to hold the weight. And why doesn't it get tangled?"

"Why, Dad?"

"Ah, they knew what they were doing in England in 1842," he said enthusiastically. "The metal's fine but strong, an alloy. And the oversized drum keeps the links straight."

"Ah," I agreed, not fully understanding this. Now I wonder if he really gave me adequate explanation. He may have been just sketching things, assuming I wasn't ready yet to understand his craft. "Are you coming to the game?"

I was playing little league that year and, like any son, wanted my father to watch me play.

"Of course, I'll be there. When is that?"

"It's 4:30, like always."

"Ah, I'll be there."

76

But he wasn't, of course.

You see, for all his love of clocks, Samuel Clark was careless about punctuality. Sometimes late, sometimes early, he could not be counted on to be where he was supposed to be when he was scheduled to be there.

To some degree, this was consistent with his clock collection, if not with timekeeping. Because each clock was made differently, you see, no one time ruled at Quixote's. Coocoos came out of their hideaways and announced the hour before, during, and after the grandfather clocks chimed the appropriate number of times. Alarms sounded, bells rung, buzzers hummed on and off for up to ten minutes at the top of the hour, while lesser dings, bongs, and tweets asserted different arrivals of the quarter-, half-, and three-quarter hours. It could be dizzying.

So extended were the periods of time's passing in our store that some customers shied away from Quixote's, patronizing Fairfield or Show Me Jewelers, where things were synchronized, orderly, consistent. Still, my father's genial manner and consistently low markup sustained his business.

Dad's casual approach to time's measurement extended to money matters also. That is, he would often take less than what was written on the price tag for individual items, especially if you were buying more than one thing. He would listen to stories of hard times and make adjustments, accept an offer that was close but not quite on the money (so the speak).

My mother claimed I was being unfair to link Dad's casual approach, the refusal to fix himself to any absolute, with his accidental death. Maybe she was right. But, confused and hurt as I was at the time, I couldn't dissociate his character from his destiny. Even now, whenever I'm reminded of the event, my gut reaction is to regret his ability to elude the fixed frames of reference that govern society-- structured time and place.

He was driving, you see, up Main Street at approximately the speed limit. Approximately synchronized with the four stoplights that alternated east/west with north/south traffic. Watching, approximately, where he was going when the Fairfield Sanitation Department truck flattened the side of his car that had just passed into the intersection through a red light.

Janet's Story VII: *A Vision*

Well, this Freddy Sills was a bit cocky, I thought! Assuming that I'd be looking for someone to enter my life, that he was a special person destined to come back into my world. Still, he was kind of cute, and I chuckled at his parting sally.

I recorded his appearance at my father's office as another sign that new things were now possible for me in this summer between my sophomore and junior years of college. A bottle with a message had popped up in my spring, inspiring me to learn about the past. Now this young man had popped back into my neighborhood, suggesting that I didn't necessarily need to return to Brad Whitaker for romance. There were, as they say, many fish in the sea (or, as I say, in the spring water).

I pursued Lucy Rivers Johns' story later that same day, researching the family in Phipps' County Public Library. Unfortunately, I didn't learn much more than I had put together from the letter in the bottle and Mrs. Anderson's account. Books about Missouri in the last century gave Luther Johns and his business a significant role in the early settlement of the area. The decline of Cold Spring Iron Works after the Civil War was acknowledged also as a consequence of changes in the industry.

Where the family went after they left Missouri, however, was not mentioned in any source I could find. I guess that's one more bit of proof that the winners write history. Still, I stumbled upon an intriguing story that might, I felt, be related to Lucy's. It involved the famous outlaw James family.

Frank and Jesse were legendary bank robbers from our area, hiding out in caves all over the territory, especially Meramec Caverns not more than fifty miles east of Fairfield along Route 66. (Just one room in those caves is said to be large enough to park 300 automobiles!) In the disorderly times after the Civil War, the James Gang (the two brothers, some cousins from the Younger family, and a few more) went on a decade-long spree of robbing stagecoaches, trains, and banks in the rugged hill country of central and eastern Missouri.

To poor folk in that time and later, I've read, they seemed to be heroes, taking from the rich to help their own people. Most of the present authorities, though, said they were a pretty nasty lot. They used hard times as an excuse for drinking and looting and shooting things up.

Their hideout in Meramec Caverns interested me because it was connected to another spring in our area, Meramec Spring. Long a place of summer outings for little communities in this area, this is one of the ten largest springs in our state. Its waters feed the Meramec River, which flows past the caverns where Jesse and his gang hung out.

Here's what caught my attention the most, a single passage in one book about "misfits" who couldn't find a place in peacetime and threatened "law abiding residents": "Meramec Spring is probably not the place Sacagawea's spirit appeared to save Oroginee Watkins from a murdering gunman. However, which of Missouri's many springs was the site of this oft-recounted miracle has never been determined."

A spring? A miracle? A woman? These things were a lot like the ingredients of my newly emerging life: Lucy Rivers Johns, my spring, myself. Perhaps I didn't have a miracle, though the bottle's magical appearance came pretty close, I thought. And I even had men--or at least a boy named Freddy--showing up.

"Do you know anything about the ghost of Lewis and Clark's Indian guide coming to the rescue of some woman at a spring?" I asked the librarian, soft-spoken, large, grandmotherly Mrs. Morriston. She had directed me to the section on local history.

"Oh, there are always stories about visions like that. You ought to ask Mrs. Anderson. Do you know her?"

"Sure, but I was wondering . . . "

"Wait a minute. Now that I think about it, there was a diary somewhere . . . " She scanned the shelves beside me. "An Osage woman. Ah, here it is, *The Diary of Mrs. Oroginee Watkins*. I think that may be in there."

I knew that the Osage people, the dominant tribe around here early in the last century, had been forced west when European settlers arrived in significant numbers after the Louisiana Purchase. Perhaps this person or her mother married a white man (a Watkins) and stayed behind.

I had read some about native American life, though it was hard in those days to find all that much that was reliable. So many of the books about Indians were written by Europeans and their descendants, and even those accounts purporting to be told in the voices of Missouri's earliest inhabitants had their words filtered and shaped by white interviewers, editors, publishers.

My inquiries into the earliest human settlements in the region brought together a limited number of verifiable facts and a lot of conjecture about Indian culture. I remained intrigued with a people who seemed to me to live in harmony with their landscape rather than trying to clear its forests, dam its rivers, cover its great stretches of prairie with concrete. Their story was, I felt, an extension of the earth's story, not an imposition on it.

Oroginee's diary told more about Indian conversion to white civilization. It covered her young life, from when she learned to write until she married a doctor and moved to Jefferson City. But in one brief section she explained her deliverance from a member of the James gang as the gift of an ancestral spirit, the Shoshone woman who took Lewis and Clark across the Rockies.

Oroginee's mother had married a trapper from Tennessee, and they raised her in the father's culture. The family settled down to farm, and she received an elementary education, hoping to teach one day. But those were still pretty unsettled days, and she was unlucky enough to encounter this outlaw, drunk and in the mood to have a woman.

Because she escaped her pursuer, Oroginee's account of the attack is subdued, even, at times, humorous. She never learned the name of her attacker, but she believed he was a member of the James gang and referred to him as "James." The appearance of Sacagawea is told with a joyful, almost religious tone.

The locale for all these events is unclear, at least to a modern reader. She writes about the farms of certain people (the Millers), the rough road from an unnamed village crossing "the stream," a store near an abandoned furnace. All I could figure at that point was that she was traveling away from the store when an unsavory character fell off his horse in front of her.

She smiled as he gathered himself from the dirt, cursing his horse for bucking him. Then he spotted Oroginee holding a basket of food and watching him struggle to his feet.

"Well, hello there, pretty lady," he'd said (or so she wrote that he said). "What're you doing here?"

"I'm on my way home." She gestured down the road over the shoulder of "James." His horse had disappeared.

"James" looked behind himself, then back at Oroginee, and past her to discover that she was traveling alone. "Why, I'm going that way too, pretty lady. Let's us walk on together."

She said no, that she was fine, and tried to skirt past him and go on her way. But he caught her by the arm and drew her to him, saying, "My, you sure do smell good! Come on with me over here behind this tree."

She broke free and ran, but he came after her. She went over a ridge, slipped and slid down a steep bank, then fell exhausted in front of a bubbling spring. It's cool water in the early evening created a mist in which she saw a figure, a young Indian woman she later identified as Sacagawea's spirit.

I had little reason, of course, to conclude that this spring was Lucy Rivers Johns' spring (except perhaps the "abandoned furnace" she mentioned) or that it was mine (just the general location of our county). But somehow I thought they might be one.

"Stand, my daughter," Sacagawea said. "And call to the man."

Oroginee did, and "James" answered from above. When she looked up toward his voice, she saw him launch himself from the cliff above and fall feet first toward her. She could see the worn heels of his boots, a rip in the crotch of his trousers, and his coat ballooning open around him. He went directly into the heart of the spring and never, she wrote, came up.

Louis's Story VII: Finder Found

The Ozark Motel was one of those quiet roadside establishments characteristic of the 1930s, 1940s, and 1950s--small individual cottages in a semicircle around an office building. Each unit and the office featured a stone face, peaked tile roof, and dark metal window frames. This particular establishment was on the edge of town, tucked back into a grove of hardwood up at the foot of a steep ridge.

During the week, when I was away from the Survey office in Fairfield, I choose a location central to my work to spend Monday through Thursday nights. I was reimbursed for lodging by the Survey and had a per diem allowance on meals. Within reason, then, I stayed wherever I wanted and ate all I needed in several dozen Missouri small towns over the fifteen weeks of summer.

Keeping careful track of my expenses for food and lodging was one of the things I prided myself on, marking each entry neatly in a ledger, which was separate from the log I kept of places I visited. I transferred the appropriate information to an official government form at the end of every week, receiving a check for that amount two weeks later. I longed for a day when Mr. Mitchell would challenge one of my claims and I could produce the detailed log I'd kept of my travel and the ledger with confirmation of

85

each expense. (That day never came, as, I guess, my reputation for precise record keeping had been established early.)

There would be no entry in log or ledger that Bobby Green had joined me for dinner one evening, nor that she returned with me to the Ozark Motel. Now, many years later, I wish I'd recorded even the dishes she ordered, precisely what we said in those moments of small talk (so awkward for me!) as we first sat down together, how it ended up that she followed me back to my room. I do, at least, remember a remarkable amount of what she said later that night.

In those summers of my youth I was insensitive to many things, including the true substance of romance. I missed the varied beauty of nature, the rich culture of the prairie and mountain people I met, the depth of my own longing. Age has given me the capacity to understand these things more fully.

As a college student on a summer job, I ate at hundreds of small-town cafes, highway diners, and favorite restaurants of traveling businessmen simply to satisfy hunger, not to appreciate fine cooking. What a loss!

The closest I came to developing a discriminating taste might have involved pie. I did like pie, and I recognized the difference between homemade and store bought. But I now know I could be fooled by the warmed-up over the just-baked, by canned instead of fresh fruit, by frozen crusts rather than those rolled out, shaped, and filled just before going into the oven.

I ate and enjoyed to greater or lesser degrees, never inquiring about the reasons for goodness or the failures that took away from quality. In fact, I suspect if I'd wondered about what accounted for such differences then, I would have been relentlessly quantitative: is that a rounded or a level quarter teaspoon of nutmeg on your apples? how many minutes exactly do you chill the dough and at what temperature? should the number of slices to let the steam out of the crust be odd or even?

Especially in country cooking, recipes and measurement are flexible. The best pies are made by feel: "a handful of flour"; "knead until soft but not sticky"; "enough to cover the bottom." Even two pies made the same day by the same person will not taste exactly alike.

Still, it was pie, as best as I can remember, that provided the transition from restaurant to motel for us, Louis the well-finder and Bobby the water-witch.

"Would you like dessert?" I suggested. We were in the kind of small, mainstreet, family restaurant you would have found in almost any mid-American small town at that time. I probably had something like hamburger steak, mashed potatoes with gravy, fresh green beans, and rolls--at a price, I bet, of no more than $1.75!

"Maybe dessert. So, you can find things?" asked Bobby. "You use official records and modern instruments?"

"Hmm?"

"Your work. That's what you do, travel about, check records, figure out where people have dug their wells."

I'd given her my basic spiel in relationship to Mr. Carter's well, explaining how I'd been fooled at first by the changes that occurred after the map I used was made.

"Yes. I think I'll have a piece of the apple pie," I tell the waitress, who has approached our table holding her pad.

"Me too," says Bobby, looking up. "But could you wrap them up to take out--paper plates?"

"Sure," the waitress says. She adds up our bills with these final items, puts them face down on the table, and turns toward the kitchen.

"To take out?" I say, raising my eyebrows.

She smiles, I think, coyly. "I'd like to hear more about your work, this well-finding business."

Now, I'd certainly read more about such overtures than experienced them! But still, I recognized the pattern: she wants to spend more time with me; it could be at the Ozark Motel.

I was glad I had straightened things up back in my room. The motel staff had made the bed and cleaned the bathroom while I was out during the day. But after work I had put logs, ledgers, and maps in neat stacks on top of the low dresser, tucked dirty clothes into a laundry bag and put that in my suitcase, hidden in the altimeter case the five post cards I mailed, one each day, to Linda from wherever I was each week of the summer.

"There're some lawn chairs back at my motel, beside the office. And a picnic table. Like to go there?"

"Sure. Tell you what, though. Let's leave my truck here, just take your car. Save gas!" she concluded with a low laugh.

I opened the door on the Survey car for Bobby and watched her hike one hip up, stretching a long leg as she swung her derriere onto the seat. Save gas! Is it, perhaps, that she doesn't want the town to know she's there, fooling around with a young man?

Events were fulfilling my prediction: she was the one arranging things. Back at the motel, though, I was able to assert a little control. Along with the lawn chairs and a picnic table, we discovered a swing in its own frame between the office and the row of cabins.

"Let's sit here," I suggested, anticipating the two of us side by side, my arm along the back of the swing, her hip against my hip.

"Sure. Do you have maps for the entire state?"

"Um, maps, yeah, I do. Although not all of them are with me, but back at the office. I just bring what I need each week for the area I'm working. You know, this week, where you are."

"I see. So, just for Arkansas County."

"Um-hum. That's all I'm interested in right now, Bobby Green country."

"But the office, where is that? Did you say Fairfield?"

For a second an image of Linda Forrester, my official girlfriend, appeared before my eyes, but I dismissed it quickly.

"Yeah, right. I'll go back there Friday, return Monday."

"Ah, another week's worth of wells to find here."

"Yes, ah, at least." There probably weren't that many, but I figured I could go slow for that one week.

"Could you do me a favor? I'd like to see a map, a topographical map--if that's what you call them--of the area just west of Fairfield. Is that your home town?"

"Yeah, it is. Each map covers about thirty square miles. Will that do it?" I wondered what she wanted to see.

"Well, yes, but bring, maybe, all the ones that show directly west, and a bit north and south along the highway. I guess that's Route 66, isn't it?"

"Route 66, yes."

"They won't take up too much space, will they?"

"Oh no, easy. I can do it, the favor. You might, though, do me some favor in return."

"Why don't you begin collecting your favor right now by kissing me," she said.

And so I did.

Janet's Story VIII:
Forebodings

When I got to the spring that evening after dinner, I tried to link up the landscape I saw with that described in Oroginee Watkins' account: road, path, cliff, spring. I also wondered if there was any evidence that I was standing by Cold Spring, Lucy Rivers Johns' place of beauty.

Of course, I had no idea what road was referred to by Oroginee, or if anything remained of the furnace she mentioned, or whether any crumbling buildings in the area could be the store she carried goods from. And there had been no map of the Cold Spring Iron Works showing a nearby spring in my library research. So I knew I was probably just speculating wildly.

I did look deep into the spring, wondering, for a moment, if the remains of "James" might pop to the surface in the same way my bottle had. Oooh, I thought, bones and teeth and maybe a belt buckle! But, of course, nothing bubbled up. I tossed a little water in the air, trying to inspire the mist in which Sacagawea had appeared and spoken to the Osage Oroginee. But that day I found evidence not of "James" or the Indian women, but of another, present day party in this area.

My spring was a couple of miles south of the four-lane Route 66. The Mother Road bypass came north around Fairfield and then west down a long sloping ridge, snaking over lesser hills and across low valleys in a further descent twenty or twenty-five miles to the Gasconade River.

You got to the spring, however, not off Route 66 but by walking or driving about a mile and three quarters out a poorly maintained gravel road south of the Circle. From our house you would go up Piney Ridge on Hill Street, down one more hill to an apparent cul de sac, then follow a narrow gravel road west that was no longer kept up by town or county. There were some scattered, rundown houses and a few abandoned trailers out that way, but I don't know that anyone lived in them. The road petered out at the base of a treeless north-south ridge marked by sharp granite outcrops.

If you then followed an old path south across the ridge, passed the ruins of a farmhouse, and wound down the far side, you would come to my spring. But you had to know it was there, as it was tucked back under an overhang.

There was also a cave further north along this ridge. The boys in our neighborhood took pride in the cold air that flowed out of the cave's mouth-- "natural air-conditioning," they said. This idea of "natural air-conditioning" probably came from family visits to Meramec Caverns, which promised travelers on nearby Route 66 a break from the heat of summer, "year-round air-conditioning." It was a steady 55-degrees winter and summer.

Stony Court's "Cold Cavern Air-conditioning," prominently advertised on Mr. Bachmann's new billboards along Route 66, had nothing to do with caves. He was building standard units into the new walls with asbestos siding after he removed the old Ozark Giraffe exterior. But he was hoping to piggyback on the advertising of Meramec Cavern's "year-round" air-conditioning that travelers would see along the highway, associating his hotel with a natural wonder, a place with history.

I still like the idea of real caves, cool, dark passages deep beneath the surface of the earth. But I no longer have a great desire to be in them. As a teenager, I'd visited Meramec and the other nearby famous Missouri cave, Onondaga. But they're both large, and the tours are commercially staged so that you don't feel claustrophobic following your guide and several dozen other tourists on a well-worn path. The boys in the Circle, though, were always teasing the girls, saying we were afraid to crawl down into our local cave with them.

"It's neat," Charles Landon might say, perhaps in the empty lot behind our house, which was often a neighborhood gathering place. "It's narrow at the entrance, but there are some nice big rooms about twenty feet in."

"Are you talking about the bat room or the spider room?" Heavy Joe Martin would ask, squinting into the distance as if he could see all the way to the cave and its dark inner chambers. He was already so large I couldn't imagine him getting into any cave smaller than Onondaga.

"Oh, all the bats are gone," Billy countered, then paused for effect. "The snakes, you know . . . "

"Ah. But the sound," continued Heavy Joe. "The sound we've heard, that hasn't stopped, has it?"

"Well now, funny you should ask. Tony said he was down there last weekend, and it was faint, but still there."

"The sound?" one of the gullible younger girls would inevitably ask.

"Yeah. It's not a whistle . . . " Charles would then give a low, drawn out whistle.

"No," Heavy Joe would say. "Maybe a sighing." He would take a deep breath and let it out slowly. "Hmmmm."

"I don't know. It's more of a . . . um . . . a crying, I guess." So Charles would cup his hands and produce a high, sad, mournful sound, someone in pain or suffering.

"I don't think anybody's trapped in there . . . ." Joe would offer.

"No, not a lost kid or anything, abandoned by her parents."

"Well, now that you mention it . . . " Charles would say. And then they would make up stories about runaway children or kids who wandered away from their yards or kidnap victims who died in the bowels of the earth.

One of the older girls would finally say something like, "If there's anything, it's probably wind going through tunnels and tiny, tiny openings deep inside, far far away."

"Yeah," another girl would confirm. "You feel that cool air coming out at the entrance, you know it has to have come from a long way off, deep underground."

"It's not a ghost, is it?" our youngest girl might then worry with a shiver. And we'd be off on another round of stories.

I don't think Freddy Sills was one of these boys tormenting girls when we were all younger. He said he'd lived in our neighborhood only a few months, and we were in kindergarten or early elementary school at the time we listened for faraway trains on the railroad tracks.

Earlier today I had seen the fully grown Freddy at my father's office. And now I was being cooled by the breeze blowing over the spring's cold water and didn't need any air-conditioning, not a cave's or Bachmann's standard units.

After a half-hour of musing at the water's edge, I was ready to head home. I'd found no more clues that might link my spring to Lucy's or to Oroginee's. For a better overall view, though, I went back up on the ridge and looked more carefully for signs of a road, a store, a furnace from seventy-five years earlier. What I found instead were red tags recently left by a survey crew.

We kids in the Circle had no idea who owned these woods west of our neighborhood, which stretched from the edge of Fairfield south of Route 66 and the Missouri Pacific railroad tracks. Was it government land, or the property of a giant timber company, or the possession of an absentee landlord in some city back east? It had never really occurred to me to ask. But I knew enough to realize that people do surveys when property is being sold, or development is being planned, or some other change is coming. And I didn't like any of those possibilities.

It had never occurred to me before this moment that this area west of town could change. The soil throughout Phipps County had been farmed out in the last century, and scrub oak woods had grown up to cover the largest area. Those who wanted to cultivate had to build up the soil with fertilizers and planned crop rotation. Most large tracts like this remained untended except for scattered residents living in older country homes and a few fancy, modern homes built by city people fleeing the rat race.

Tugging idly at one of the red tags on top of the ridge, I tried to see the outline suggested by its mates. They crossed the ridge and disappeared into woods on the far side. And behind me they dipped down to the east of the cliff over my spring. They seemed, ominously, to be drawing a circle around the favorite place of my childhood.

Louis's Story VIII: *Lost Virginity*

I recognized Bobby Green's kiss immediately as different from anything I'd ever experienced with Linda. It wasn't as if this was a roadblock I had to get around, or a way point at which I had to pause and validate my new status, or some test of my motives that couldn't be passed. No, it was an open invitation to continue to a better place.

Now, Linda had the same better place, I'm sure. It's just that she couldn't go there without first progressing through a complex series of necessary steps. The last of them, of course, was holy matrimony.

Or at least so I believed at the time.

Some years after this momentous summer in my life, I gained enough experience to reconsider Linda's character, and my own. I had been convinced for years that she was insisting on strict adherence to a social code, the mandatory sequence of stages to intimacy. But hindsight has raised the very real possibility that I was the one all along who hesitated at every advance in our relationship. A shocking possibility, to be sure, when I first confronted it.

But I know I had an addiction to precise timekeeping, deriving, at least in part, from the shock of my father's death. I had insisted on a departure from his practice, which I felt helped create the conditions for disaster. That is, I was never going to be ahead of or behind schedule in any way that might threaten my mother with a second great loss. So, perhaps unconsciously, I insisted on a deliberate order in courtship that I imposed on poor Linda, who, for all I know now, was wild with desire for me or any boy!

I was surprised when Bobby Green showed desire openly, on the swing in the Ozark Motel's courtyard and in my room shortly thereafter. But at the time I believed her to be unique, a woman absolutely out of the ordinary. It turned out, of course, that there were other reasons for her frankness and her appetite.

Back when I entered the unsteady state of puberty, I had no adult couple to serve as a model of physical relationship. Mom had been a young woman when she lost her husband, but she did not date after that or show any desire to remarry. Placing her chaste life within the context of conservative 1950s mores, I concluded that men alone needed or wanted physical intimacy.

My mother's life was restrained in many ways in the second half of my growing up. She had been working part-time with my father to hold down expenses in running the store, while keeping house the rest of the day. (There was only me at the time, but I know they had wanted, but didn't think they could afford, more children.) And she'd had a very hard time making ends meet in the early years of her widowhood.

My father had let his life insurance lapse, either because it had become a luxury he didn't think they could justify, or because it was not in his nature to follow any one clock, even a payment schedule. So he left me and my mother with only a lease on Quixote's space and a new mortgage on a small house in Fairfield Gardens. We were able to stay in our home, but Mom couldn't keep the store afloat alone.

I can understand why Mom made staying in our house the first priority, as Fairfield Gardens was a good place to finish growing up. This was--and is--a little neighborhood consisting of two horseshoe drives off state highway 77, which angles southeast from Route 66 and downtown out toward Steelville, Missouri. The horseshoes come one after the other on the north side of the road just as you're ready to leave town (town as it was in the 1950s). In the middle of each U-shape is a lane ending in a little circle of four houses--seen from above, a lollipop inside a horseshoe.

While these horseshoes weren't connected to each other by streets (except through their entrances on highway 77 to the south), the neighborhood was neatly connected by paths that slipped between houses--from the lollipop top to the outer horseshoe, from the side of one horseshoe to the side of the other. There was even a path cutting between two houses over to Belleview, which ran north from Highway 77 up to Fairfield East Elementary School and the high school. This was a cozy, close neighborhood, and my mother didn't want to have to move away from it when I was at such a vulnerable point in my life.

For a time I maintained an elaborate set of maps of Fairfield Gardens, using colored pencils to differentiate street from highway from path from driveway. Drawings of each house accurately reflected the building it represented and was marked by the name of the family who lived there. Wooded areas were a darker green than grassy places; fire hydrants, drainage ditches, manholes, telephone poles, culverts and fences were precisely marked. I updated the set weekly.

At the time I was in college, my mother and I still lived at 33 Fairfield Gardens, third house from Highway 77 on the outside of the second horseshoe. And I would be there this Friday night, telling my mother of the week's events and calling Linda Forrester to arrange our going out for a Coke that evening.

With Bobby Green's tongue gently parting my lips in front of the Ozark Motel, however, I wondered what I would be able to say to either woman. I did, at least, think of something to say to Bobby in one of our gasping pauses.

"Would you, ahh, like to go inside?"

"I'd like that. As we walk, let me tell you about my great aunt."

"Your great aunt?" This was to me a most unnecessary *non sequitur*.

"She was quite a woman, a big time philanthropist early in this century."

"Oh?" I put the key in the lock, turned it and the doorknob, then opened the door for Bobby to go first. Scanning the room over her shoulder, I was again pleased to see its basic order, things in appropriate places.

"Her mother was born in Missouri, but she moved to New York, and eventually married a partner in one of the big Wall Street firms." As Bobby walked, she kicked off her sandals. She took my hand, turned to face me, and led me backwards toward the bed.

"So she inherited money and . . . uh . . . then used it . . . um . . . for the public good?"

Those pauses in my conversation were inspired by Bobby's wrapping both arms around my neck, kissing me with, I thought, both pleasure and enthusiasm. Then she pulled me down with her onto the bed.

"Let me finish this story when we're finished with each other," she said. I agreed and began traveling down the path I'd so long imagined, the slow, careful journey I'd forecast I would take with Linda Forrester. I didn't, however, direct this journey, which was not, of course, slow. Bobby rolled on top of me and ran the show, beginning to end, wham-bam.

Now, I'd heard the phrase "lost my virginity" many times in high school and in my two years of college. I'd been taught that a girl's "loss" of virginity was sad, a subtraction of something important from her identity. Men, on the other hand, "lost" theirs in a positive way, vigorously casting aside a burdensome feature of childhood in order to appear in a fully formed state.

As it happened to me that warm summer night deep in the Ozarks, this loss of my virginity, I felt I'd

101

been subtracted from where Bobby had profited. She took from me, and I had no power to lessen her in the slightest. Not, however, that I wanted to. But this simply wasn't what I had expected.

Well, too, it all happened very fast. As much as I had anticipated this experience, planning to linger over it with care, the whole thing, I suspect, didn't eclipse a single minute, sixty seconds. I would come to see before too long that all this wasn't bad, but it was sure a surprise to one innocent twenty-year-old!

Another thing was probably true of me then: beside being ferociously innocent, I had, really, almost no sense of humor. I guess, as busy as I'd always been arranging things, scheduling events, and keeping records of it all, I also kept in check the general human tendency to laugh. So when Bobby felt what was happening to me and broke into a delighted peal of laughter, I was yet again taken completely by surprise.

Janet's Story IX: Hillbillyville

I had so much to ask Sophie Anderson about, not just the past but also the present. She still kept abreast of local affairs, and she might know, if anyone did, what was going on in the woods around my spring. Since her house was only a few blocks from my father's office, I decided to walk over there the next day on my lunch hour and see what light she could shed on this development.

Now, I've told you that Mrs. Anderson was a bit of an eccentric. But perhaps anyone who lives to her age is going to develop some unusual traits! Still, her house had assumed its atypical character decades ago, after she lost her husband.

Always fond of pets, she'd decided as a new widow to take up the breeding of small animals like mice, rabbits, and gerbils for laboratory use. She insisted on selling to research programs that would observe, not sacrifice, her creatures. And she would not supply anyone with immature animals, saying that God's non-human creatures should have the chance to reach adulthood without undue interference from us.

Anyway, when you rang the doorbell at Mrs. Anderson's modest brick house, you expected to have to wait patiently for her to appear, as she was always extricating herself from feeding the animals, washing their cages, immunizing them, or treating special cases. And more times than not, she had furry bundles in each hand, along her shoulder, underfoot.

Since she'd been doing this for over forty years, her grounds, garage, and the house itself had been transformed into an animal production facility. Food was stored in a spare bedroom, the garage was a packaging station for receiving and shipping out orders, the pantry held medical supplies, cages littered the basement, the enclosed porch, and much of the yard.

She always saved a few members of each generation in order to breed new animals. And she could tell you the ancestry of each group, the traits she'd hoped to develop, and often the role the newest ones would play in research. Since she'd been doing this for over four decades, she had records of more generations than the Old Testament!

In a number of ways, Sophie Anderson was a person after my own heart. Having lived a long time herself, she had the long view of history. With her animals she looked back over many generations to beginnings, developments, conclusions. She also could see forward to probable results. I guess that's why she sometimes claimed to have special sight, reading the future.

In a similar way, I had taken up my bottle from the past and its even more compelling letter by an early Missourian and now wanted to find out what had become of that woman's dreams. I wondered if my own life would take up and continue this earlier story. But I asked first about those red tags.

"It looks like they've surveyed out there, a great big area. Are they planning to build something, or is this just checking old boundaries?"

"Come with me," said Mrs. Anderson and took me by the hand.

"Where are we . . . ?" I asked, but I knew from past experience that she wouldn't say until she was ready. Again, this lady enjoyed the prerogatives of her age.

She led me past stacked cages of gray gerbils in the living room, golden hamsters in the dining room, and speckled, larger creatures I couldn't identify in the pantry out to the back yard.

"I want you to meet Janet," she said.

"I am Janet."

"I know, dear. This is Janet, the porcupine."

I saw a large cage, perhaps ten cubic feet, in the middle of which a single tree stood in a big clay pot. There was pine straw all over the floor and a large pan of water in one corner, but I didn't see Janet.

"In the tree," offered Mrs. Anderson. And then I spotted the beast holding a pine cone and gnawing contentedly at it. The porcupine was about the size of a small terrier and had quills several inches long.

"Ah," I said. "He . . . she? . . . looks very much at home."

"She is. She was a baby when some hunters found her in a box trap set for squirrels. Her parents must have given up trying to free her and were nowhere in the area, so the guys brought her in to me. She's become quite domesticated, haven't you, little one?"

"Are you letting her grow up so you can send her to a lab?"

"Oh, no. She'll go back to the wild in a few more weeks. That's what I wanted to talk to you about."

"The wilds? Where my spring is?"

"Where you are. Not in the wilds yet."

"I think I'm confused."

"Sit down, dear." She gestured to a bench beside Janet's cage, and I did as she asked. "You see, each stage of life has its place, its environment."

"OK."

"For this Janet," she pointed toward the cage. "For this Janet her first environment was the woods where her parents lived. Now she's in a second place, here with me, protected. But in time she'll have to move on to a third setting, some woods without her parents there to find food and take care of her."

"I see. And if those woods change, because of development, she'll have to find another place to be?"

"That's right. And that's what's happening to you. Your place of childhood is going to change. I know you've always loved that spring. It's been a great place to run away to, a secret hideaway. But this happens to all of us, change."

"So now I have to leave?"

"The spring itself is leaving, or it will be covered over. Janet, a huge amusement park is going to be built out that way."

"An amusement park? Disneyland?" This was a mecca for many Fairfield families in those days, inspiring them to drive 2,000 miles on Route 66 to show children Mickey and Donald and Goofy.

"Yes, a theme park, but not a Disney one. From what they tell me, the entrance to the park will come off Route 66, and the whole thing will stretch over several square miles. There will be theaters and restaurants and hotels and rides."

"Adventureland. Fantasyland."

"Mmm-hmm. But you're moving on. You're at college now, and you'll probably want to go somewhere, to some big city, teach history, maybe find a husband. You won't miss it so much."

"Mrs. Anderson," I said after a pause. "What kind of amusement park are they building? I mean, what's its theme?"

"Oh, well, does it really matter? You'll be graduated from college and out on your own by the time it really gets going."

"I just want to know."

"Yes, I see. Well, it's going to be called, I think, 'Hillbillyville.' It will feature mountain folk sitting on cabin porches and singing simple ballads, little plays about two families feuding over where they put their moonshine stills, hillbilly children playing hooky from school to go fishin'."

"Oh, horrible! That's not the way people really live."

"I know. But these are stereotypes that sell, I'm afraid. People will come to be amused. And these parks are all about making money, pandering to the public's taste."

"Who's doing it?"

"Some bigwigs back East apparently. They've bankrolled it, but local firms will get a lot of business. It will be a real boom to Fairfield and Phipps County."

I did see that it would help people like Mr. Bachmann with Stony Court. That should mean more work for people my age like Freddy Sill. But it wasn't natural. It would transform the old landscape worse than Lake of the Ozarks was bloating and deforming the Osage River. This would take the spring I thought might be Lucy Rivers Johns' spring, perhaps the place of Sacagawea's magical appearance.

"I know one thing about a porcupine," I said to Mrs. Anderson, pointing to the other Janet. "Most people think they're passive when attacked, just rolling up in a ball no dog or predator could bite. But they're not just passive. They swing that tail and plant those quills. Angry, they can be vicious."

"I know dear."

"Well, about this theme park, Mrs. Anderson--I'm angry!"

Louis's Story IX:
Inheritance

I said earlier that Bobby Green pulled me down on the bed at the Ozark Motel. What I didn't say then was that I felt as if the bed had opened up and I had begun an unexpectedly pleasant freefall.

Her laugh of delight at my lack of control brought my feeling of gentle floating to a halt, but it was not a hard landing. I was remarkably satisfied at this entry into sexual maturity. I was, however, more than a bit tongue-tied.

"Well . . . I . . . that . . . whoosh!"

Lying on her back beside me, she patted my arm. "Very nice," she said simply.

Then, much, much too late, I began to think about what I should have done when we entered the motel room: gotten a condom out of my suitcase!

"Um . . . I . . . I hope this is the, er, the right time of the month for you?"

"Oh, that's nothing. It doesn't matter." She had clasped her hands behind her head on the pillow and was gazing absentmindedly at the ceiling.

"Nothing! But . . . shouldn't we worry . . . ?"

"I have an I.U.D., Louis. Do you always use 'Louis,' by the way, or do some people call you 'Lou'?"

"It's Louis. Louis."

I'd read about intrauterine devices, so I understood this was an effective method of birth control. What the actual piece of plastic looked like, how it was used, where exactly inside a woman's reproductive anatomy it went were mysteries to me. How they worked to prevent pregnancy wasn't a bit clearer. When I consider how little I knew about the inner workings of women--physical, psychological, mental, emotional--that's no surprise.

In the course of this evening with an obviously more experienced woman, I came to realize considerable irony in my situation. A well-finder, I had been seeking openings in the earth across the Show Me state all summer, as well as for three months the previous year. Each well was an entry into the secrets of Mother Earth, the sandstone, dolomite, limestone, shale, oil, water that, in a very real sense, made up the land I lived on. Plotting its location on a map, I'd developed further a grid of surface features to link with what lay underground.

Similarly, I'd sought over the same time span a way into a woman's inner self, but in the crudest possible manner, through sexual penetration. But the goal had been getting there, not understanding where that place was, what a woman is. Perhaps it was only fair that, when sex finally came, I was more swallowed up by it than able to break through to the secret heart of things.

I'd like to rationalize my slowness of perception by linking it to my father's example, though I know that wouldn't be entirely fair. Still, he was always looking into clocks, laying bare their machinery. And this posited an assertion that, once each part was identified and seen in relationship to others, the entire timepiece could be understood. It was if he went in by the little opening the coo-coo popped out of and captured the bird in its lair. So I might have been adopting his strategy and trying to understand women by gaining access to their inner workings

No boy wants to know, of course, the inner workings of his mother, especially how she conceived, gestated, gave birth to him. When I had finally put together the complete picture of human reproduction (from buddy talk in a neighborhood tree house, overheard comments of older boys on the school playground, and some instructions in a few agricultural guidebooks), my mother was without the man who played the necessary role in producing me. So I did not do well perceiving the nature of women, especially a woman with the force I'd found in Bobby Green.

I'd met another woman whose inner life was initially hidden from me last summer when I was well-finding. I thought of her as "the Peculiar old lady," not because she was strange but because I'd met her in the hamlet of Peculiar, south of Kansas City.

It's flat there, an eastern portion of the great plains. The streets are straight, and you can identify the precise edge of town by the beginning of cornfields that stretch to the horizon, dotted here and there with the pumps of working oil wells. A person from the Ozark foothills, I assumed the people of Peculiar were as uncomplicated as the town's level layout around a small central square.

(I'd similarly assumed Bobby Green was a simple country girl, but she wasn't acting the part.)

I found the house I was looking for in Peculiar easily enough, on one of those streets that marked the town limits. While the door behind the screen was open and windows raised at the bottom to get the late afternoon breeze, there were no sounds--no radio, not a sewing machine, nothing clattering in the kitchen. My loud knocking, however, produced from the dark interior a stooped elderly lady.

I wanted to confirm my well quickly and keep moving, aware of the altimeter's drifting in time and the necessity of returning to a bench mark every hour. But the Peculiar old lady had many questions. She insisted on fixing me a glass of iced tea, on our sitting on her front porch for "just a bit," on her asking me about my family, school, the job of well-finding. I realized my appearance was filling one small part of a long day for her.

She lived by herself, having survived two husbands and eight children. Her grandchildren were so scattered she didn't know their present whereabouts. She'd even outlived her contemporaries in this town where she'd been born and spent all her days, so she endured many hours, many days completely alone.

Probably because I knew the loss of my father, I stayed well past the time I should have and had to take a second elevation the next day, trusting that the ground a block away from her house was not significantly higher or lower. But I didn't forget the Peculiar old lady.

"So, this great aunt?" I asked Bobby Green in the Ozark Motel, more to take my mind away from how little I knew about women than to learn about her family.

"Yes, the wealthy benefactor. She was always fond of me."

"That's nice."

"In fact, I'm in her will. But I think my East Coast relatives are trying to get around it."

"Is it money? I mean, those funds she gave to charities?"

"No, it's property. Considerable acreage here in Missouri."

"Ah." And a light went on for me here. "Up near Fairfield? Is that why you need those maps, to see where the property is in relation to everything else?"

"Yes, but it's more than that, I think. I'll need some help researching court records, titles and the like. You might know something about those things, from your looking for wells?"

"Yeah, I know some things. But it sounds like to me you're going to need a lawyer."

"That's no problem. I am a lawyer."

"You're . . . ? A lawyer. I thought you were a water-witch, a local, um, girl."

"I am a 'local girl'," she said with a stiff-lipped grin. "But I haven't lived my whole life here. Right now, I'm just home for a while before deciding what I want to do with my law degree."

"You have the degree. Say, ah, how old are you?"

"Twenty-six back in May. How about you?"

"Well, I'm . . . uh . . . just, um, twenty-one." I lied here, of course, as I wouldn't be twenty-one until October. But I was completely taken aback by these revelations--her sexual experience, her education, her age. I had completely misinterpreted "Flowery Dress," as I'd first called her, when, out of the corner of my eye, I noticed her attractive figure as she stepped up into her pickup truck in the little village of Lost Spring. She was hardly some innocent young backcountry thing.

"Where did you go to law school?" I asked

"St. Louis University, same place I was an undergraduate."

OK, so great! My rural farm girl is really a city woman, intelligent, educated, and, I guess, potentially wealthy if she can claim this inheritance. This had not been a good week for Louis, the clever detective of well-finding fame. I would be lucky if I could find my way back to Fairfield on Friday!

Janet's Story X: Luther Johns's "Fabulous Fountain"

For the next few days I carried my anger about Hillbillyville around with me, a chip on my shoulder. I bothered my father and his downtown professional colleagues, complained to my mother and her social set, accosted my peers getting ice cream at the drug store soda fountain. I vowed to find out who was behind this project, raise the consciousness of Fairfield to the indignity of the whole idea, and rally the good guys to the cause of saving my spring. I was angry.

An initial calmer step in my campaign was to return to Phipps County Library and read more about the history of town and county, trying to confirm our identity as an enterprising, productive people who respected the land on which we lived. We wanted to continue contributing to the country's postwar growth, I thought, not turn ourselves into a giant tourist attraction for East- and West-coast vacationers who would reach us traveling down Route 66.

Of course, the first evidence I found involved agriculture, our region's traditional production of corn, soybeans, and fruit; hogs, cattle, and turkey. It's true that early use of the land had been wasteful, with little attention to crop rotation, replanting of forests, careful breeding of livestock. But recent farming was more scientific, carefully planned, in tune with national governmental programs.

Mining has also always been a significant Missouri industry, with lead, copper, silver, and zinc being most profitable. There is oil and some gas along the western border of the state, and coal is found in the northeast corner. So, the Show Me State wasn't just an empty space that could be turned into a fictional landscape, a playground for out-of-staters who would belittle the education and culture of locals.

My reading also turned up a surprise for me, the story of Luther Rivers Johns' "Fabulous Fountain." It wasn't in an account of the founding and development of Cold Spring Iron Works, but in an overview of technological advances that had expanded productivity in the last century.

I'd learned before that this early industrial pioneer carried a special invention with him from his early days in Tennessee, a pump that pushed water uphill using only the earth's gravity as an engine. To immigrant homesteaders and Indians it seemed a magical machine. Well, it did to me too, until I found this detailed explanation of its operation.

The device was originally designed by the hot air balloonists, the Montgolfier brothers, in France. The region they lived in was not unlike the Ozarks, limestone plateaus with rivers in deep gorges. But the idea sprang up in other places too and spread quickly.

While Johns' Fabulous Fountain, a variation on the Montgolfier's design, would be supplanted by small and mobile steam and gas engines later in the century, his discovery answered an ancient human problem: how to irrigate economically portions of dry land that couldn't be reached by simply diverting existing streams.

"This is the kind of thing I'm talking about!" I told Sophie Anderson later that day. "American ingenuity, that's what settled this area. We should celebrate our achievements, not let them be plowed under and covered with pavement."

"Tell me about this fountain. I still don't understand it." She was looking at the diagram copied from one of the books I had been reading.

"And another thing, it didn't make a mess, like so many new things do." I was thinking of the furnace Johns would also construct, that did dump waste into Missouri's riverways. I liked the fountain of his early career much more than the iron smelting business that actually made his money.

"I don't see what drives the water up the pipe." Mrs. Anderson was still puzzling over my drawing.

"OK, here. Let me explain. It's really just gravity and air pressure."

I had drawn a horizontal pipe lying under the surface of a stream, the left end lower than the right. The left end turned up in a curve and was open there, so that water could flow from one end of the pipe (on the right) to the other (the left). A one-way valve in the top of the middle of the pipe led to a vertical chamber above. Stream or river water entered at the right end of the apparatus through a small feed pipe.

"The water flows in here," I said, pointing to where the feed pipe opened into the end of the larger one. "Then, see this cannonball?" It was almost the same size as the inside of the big pipe and lay at the bottom of the little curve at the left end. "As the water enters the main pipe, it pushes the cannonball up into the other end. The cannonball blocks the exit here on the left, where water would otherwise flow out."

"OK," Mrs. Anderson agreed. "So now the pressure of water still coming in on the right pushes open the one-way valve in the middle on top?"

"Right. Water is pushed up into this chamber here," I pointed, "which had just been full of air. When the air pressure in the chamber builds up enough, it shoots the water out of the chamber through this delivery pipe." I pointed to a small pipe on the side of the upper chamber, which actually then delivered the water to the higher elevation you were trying to reach.

"Then the cannonball rolls back down, starting the whole thing over again," I concluded.

"How clever! And simple."

"Yes, that's it. See, there are lots of farms down in the Ozarks with high ridges that go dry when there's not enough rain. Especially fruit orchards--apples, peaches, pears--they can't make it without some irrigation."

"And Johns' Fountain worked for them?"

118

"It sure did. Not just pumping water to the house and barn, but to hilltop storage tanks. There are so many rushing streams in the mountains, fed by springs, you can find a good source in lots of places."

"And it doesn't burn coal or wood or require anyone to dam up the river."

"It's mostly just a pipe running up the hillside. It works on the gravity pulling the water downstream in the creek. Then the air pressure created in this chamber pushes it up the delivery pipe. Quiet, continuous, reliable except in the driest of weathers. And then nothing else would work either."

"Well now, I have an idea. Maybe you could get the people making this amusement park, this Hillbillyville, to make a little play about the Johns pump. Sort of like a museum piece, where people would learn this history."

"Oh, Mrs. Anderson, they won't want to do that. Entertainment is going to win out over education. They'll want corn cob pipes, barefoot illiterates spitting on the porch, incestuous families eating possum stew. We've got to stop them."

"Janet, I think you're exaggerating here. And you don't know what you're up against," Mrs. Anderson said, turning more serious. "There are powerful people behind this project. And more folks than you think are going to be in favor of Hillbillyville."

"But they don't know what they're losing. It's our heritage, it's who we are."

I think I knew even then, though, that Sophie Anderson was right. I was a little person thinking of taking on the big guys. I was young, female, inexperienced. And if I had known then what I was truly up against, I believe I would have gone back to the University of Missouri for my junior year--or married Brad Whitaker and spent the rest of my days having babies, baking cookies, gossiping over the backyard fence about whose husband was cheating on his wife now. But I didn't.

I went after Hillbillyville like I was Joan of Arc, an invincible saint--who was eventually martyred! That last part at least didn't apply to me, thankfully, though I think I can say I got burned more than once during my crusade. It will be up to the present generation, I guess, to decide if what I've devoted my life to--Route 66 Spring--was a fool's errand or a gift to America. I made my decisions, and I lived by them. And I don't regret any one of them.

Louis's Story X: Prospects

Returning to Fairfield at the end of that week, I was a lot like a dog with his tale between his legs. While it was true I had accurately located some Arkansas County wells for the Missouri Geological Survey, I'd also found a lot of holes in my vision of the world. I knew little about women, certainly Roberta Green--lawyer, water witch, lover.

This primary discovery led me to wonder how much I understood about other women, like my mother, the widow, a person I had taken for granted all of my life. And at home that evening I learned that I didn't know my old girl friend very well either. When I called to see if Linda wanted to go out, she said no.

"I think, Louis, I think we need to take a break."

"A break? From each other?"

"Yes. It's just that you want some things I can't, um, do right now. And you're gone all week anyway. So why don't you, you know, call me after a while. Maybe in a few weeks."

In retrospect this all makes perfect sense. At the time I assumed that she just meant I wanted sex and she didn't. Now I know she didn't want me. In the fall I would learn she had already been taking lunch breaks (from her job as clerk at the Banner Hotel) with Martin Sanders, the high school band conductor whom she would later marry, the future father of her six children.

121

My ego, bruised in my encounters with Lost Spring residents--Mrs. Green, old man Carter, Roberta--probably needed to dress up Linda's dissatisfaction with me as a failure in her own perception. She didn't see the value of the man who had been so steady since high school, I concluded.

And perhaps it was time to expand my own horizons, look for those famous other fish in the sea. After all, a 26-year-old lawyer had just slept with me! (I repressed the fact that she had wanted my help in researching property ownership.)

Unfortunately, there was no one else in Fairfield I could call on Friday for a date that weekend, so I decided to pursue Bobby Green's request about maps of the Fairfield area. In fact, I would go one step further, actually take a look at the region she wanted to know about.

I could get material from the office Saturday morning, check in at the courthouse about recent real estate transactions in the area, be prepared to surprise Bobby with more than she expected when I returned to Arkansas County next week. I didn't anticipate meeting a young woman out in the woods off Route 66, however. But this was another surprise encounter that would shape the course of my life for many years to come.

What I learned from my brief research effort was that the only current large property transaction involved an out-of-state development company, which was acquiring a 100-acre tract west of Fairfield. The land was part of a large estate that included property in New York City, Paris, and Phipps' County.

At present there was no access to most of it, but an old forest service roadbed off Route 66 allowed me to hike into the area on Saturday afternoon. It was a beautiful stretch of land, a spacious, rolling plateau covered mostly in scrub oak bordered to the south by several high ridges. The shape of the property was marked by the red tags of a recent survey.

Reaching the first of those high ridges, I looked back over the way I'd come. It reminded me of the view I'd had at the top of Walnut Ridge on my way to Old Man Carter's place. While not as varied and wild as that spot, these rolling hills had their own gentle beauty. In the farther distance I could see The Mother Road, winding its way west.

In fact, the scene was giving me unexpected satisfaction. I assumed it could all belong to my new friend Bobby, and it matched her easy self-confidence. I imagined myself connected to her and this place in some vague continuing relationship. There was harmony and a deep order in the feeling.

My reverie was broken by a feminine chuckle, "Hoo-hoo, ho-ho, hee-hee, haaaaah," and an observation. "You look like you're wondering where in the world you are!"

It came, I found on turning around, from a girl about my own age, who must have come up from the valley past this ridge. She was holding a small object in one hand, perhaps a stone. The smile on her face told me that I did indeed look a bit goofy.

"Oh, hi. It is my first time out here, but I'm not completely lost. I was struck by how nice it looks. Hmm, do I know you?"

"I'm not sure, but you seem familiar, too. You from Fairfield?"

"Yes. You?"

"Graduated high school here two years ago. I go to Stephens now, in Columbia."

"Me too. Not Stephens," I acknowledged at another of her laughs. "Not Stephens, but the university. And I was in the same class here. I'm Louis Clark." I didn't put out my hand, as women generally didn't shake hands then and her right hand was still closed on something.

"I'm Janet Masters. You were in our class. That's odd. I don't place you, at least not yet."

"Oh, we were in a different set," I admitted. Now I realized who this was, the doctor's daughter. Very pretty, very popular. Linda had been my only girlfriend, and she was behind me in school. We didn't socialize with other couples, and I tended to spend a lot of evenings at home with my mother.

"Well, what are you doing out here in the woods? This is a place I come to a lot." She pointed back toward town. "My neighborhood's not so far that way."

"I'm working. In the summer I locate wells for the Missouri Geological Survey." I held up my topographical map.

She studied my face for a moment. "Hey, now I remember: didn't I meet you once, at a mixer at Stephens. Geology major, you told me about sink holes and underground rivers."

"Was that you? Wow! I remember that. It was loud, though, the music, and not much light. That's

124

probably why we didn't recognize each other. And I'm not a geology major. This is just a summer job."

"I see. You're working on Saturday?" She gestured to the map and the altimeter dangling from one fist.

"Well, not usually. This is unofficial, for a friend."

"Were you part of the surveying here?" She gestured toward the closest string of red flags.

"No, um, it's . . . that's someone else. I think this land's changing hands. And I know someone who might be involved, and she asked me to scout it out."

"They tell me this is going to be turned into a giant amusement park. All the trees cut down, everything landscaped, the creeks and springs put underground, in culverts and such."

"Whoa! That's a big change, not a good change." I looked again at the panorama before me.

"You know about locusts?" the girl asked.

"Locusts? Well, I know what they are, how you see their shells attached to trees."

"Yes, after seventeen years cicada nymphs climb up out of the ground, grab hold of the bark with their feet, split their own shells down the back, then climb out in their mature forms." She opened her hand, showing one of those shells.

"When I was younger," she went on, "I worried that these shells would come back to life. All dry and stiff, something would happen and they'd run up the tree, or start to fly."

"I see." I didn't, of course.

"They're the way all of nature is, don't you think? Always changing, but through cycles and really unchanging. It's only mankind that changes things permanently. We tear down mountains and widen rivers and fix things just to suit us."

"I guess you're right."

"Well, that's what's going to happen to this place," she said, pointing, "unless someone does something about it." She paused. "And I just might be that person."

Seeing a sudden new intensity in her face, I thought she might be indeed. What I didn't know then, of course, was that so might I.

Interlude:
Missouri Legends II

The old story of two boys willing to risk death for each other in the underground river continues to inspire new generations in the Show Me State. It features a model friendship, cure from a fatal disease, and a miraculous escape.

Neighborhood pals in the small town of Holman's Bridge early in the Depression years, Doug and Tommy did everything together, encouraged by their ravenous consumption of boys' adventure stories. They were sure there were bad men about-- probably some escaped from the state prison in nearby Jefferson City, the state's capitol--and that, at some point in the future, someone would call on them to save the town.

They might have to scale a water tower, confront a lion somehow loose on a main street, or rescue a child from a burning building. Like the literary characters that inspired them, they would write secret codes to handle difficult cases. A clever trap into which a dangerous criminal would fall might have to be painstakingly constructed in the dark of night. Or their precise knowledge of the local terrain could be the key to locating a lost treasure.

Doug was more the brains of the two, and Tom the better athlete (though neither was stupid or without physical ability). Living on the same street in a respectable part of town, they did well in school, went to church and Sunday school, believed in the importance of community, the spirit of Holman's Bridge. They had also sworn an oath never to abandon each other. Spitting in their palms and clasping hands, they recited the oath also learned from books, "all for one, one for all."

In their imagined exploits they enjoyed the appreciation of young girls, parents, and town officials. In the end, each was happy to escape in one piece the trial that made them famous.

With several other kids from town, they were exploring one of the famous caves in their area on a dry autumn day, imagining that this was the hideout of notorious bank robbers. Tom, leading the way several hundred yards deep into a hillside, approached a well-known drop-off above an underground stream. The boys carried flashlights, with matches and sticks wrapped in tar soaked rags to use as torches in real emergencies.

"Stay back from the edge," Doug told his friend. "Remember it was slimy the last time we were here."

"It's not bad now," responded Tom, though he still stepped cautiously. The beam from his flashlight played on the water below. "The water's so low down there, I almost think we could follow it."

All the boys of Holman's Bridge--and the men too--speculated about the stream, where it came from and where it went. This spot was less than five miles from the mighty Missouri River, and many insisted that was the stream's destination. Others thought the direction suggested by the stream's crossing the large room was west, toward the also substantial Osage River.

"Let me look too," said Doug. "I think my flashlight has the stronger beam."

He reached Tom's side, resting a hand on his friend's shoulder, and directed a light toward the point where water rushed under a ledge. The rest of the gang moved forward to look also.

Over the years people had launched small wooden boats, glass bottles, and sealed metal cans full of air down the stream, waiting for them to be discovered somewhere. They attached notes or labels indicating the sender, the date, and the place where they were launched, but no word ever came back.

Later Doug said Tom seemed to startle at his side, and the next thing he knew there was a splash where his friend entered the water twenty-five feet below. Tom had fallen into the stream.

Without thinking, Doug jumped too, loyal to their pact of sticking together. He didn't have time to consider, he said. He just did what they'd always said they would do.

The other friends couldn't believe what was happening. They saw--or thought they saw--both boys disappear under the ledge in the swift racing water.

Tom and Doug had lost their flashlights in the fall, of course, and the torches. But they found each other in the rushing water, dark as it was so far underground. Doug caught Tom's left hand with his right, and they kept that grip as, with their other

hands, they swam and pushed off the rocky sides of the stream's channel.

Fortunately, rainfall had been light all summer, and the water was down. The boys had space above the water's surface to breath, though in places their heads scraped the stone above them. The current was also swift, so they couldn't really control their progress. They were battered on all sides, but always kept their hold on each other.

Afterwards they couldn't say how long was their underground journey, only that they were barely able to continue a swimming motion when they shot out of a cliff in the midst of a small waterfall that ended in the Missouri River. And if the pilot of a barge making its slow way upstream hadn't spotted them crashing into the river, they would probably have drowned in their exhaustion. He later sent word to the town, where Tom and Doug's buddies had raised an alarm.

It was surely a miracle, townspeople said. But it wasn't the only one, as they learned several weeks later.

While Tom continued to insist he had just slipped from the ledge above the river, Doug couldn't quite believe him. Both boys had been to this spot dozens of times, and they knew to be careful. And they were steady, right beside each other, just before Tom went over. Doug felt his friend had deliberately jumped. But why?

The answer came when they were anticipating their next adventure.

"I heard there's an eagle's nest up on Taylor's Ridge," said Tom when they were completely recovered from the cuts and bruises sustained in their underground whitewater trip. "Are you OK to go see?"

"OK? Sure. I wasn't any more beat up than you."

"Yeah," agreed Tom. But then he lowered his voice and said, "I know about the other thing."

"The other thing?" Doug was mystified.

"The blood thing. You're dying right?"

Apparently, Tom had overheard the doctor talking to the druggist on a street corner several weeks before the accident, and he believed Doug was dying of leukemia. For a few days, so had Doug's family, as a blood test came back positive after their boy had been sick for a week. It turned out that the doctor misread the test, and a second, done for confirmation, relieved all concerned. Doug soon got well, but Tom thought it was just a matter of time before his friend would collapse.

Tom had trouble conceptualizing Doug's condition. He was unable to picture the injury leukemia would inflict that would destroy his body. Dying from a gunshot would have made sense, or being hit by a train created a scene Tom could understand. What he overheard Doug's doctor saying involved an invisible flaw present throughout the system, and he couldn't get it to make sense in his mind.

In school he had learned about blood's circulation through the body, oxygen necessary to life delivered to every cell. The schematic diagram hanging on a stand in their classroom of a man--his legs apart, his arms raised--showed the major organs being supplied by the heart. Lungs, kidneys, stomach were all connected by the flow of fluid, all part of a single integrated system.

That some blood cells in the blood, invisible to the human eye, would race through Doug's arms and legs causing fatal damage was unimaginable. A silent, invisible killer.

Still, Tom accepted the fact that Doug would drop dead one day soon. He planned to make that end heroic by appearing to fall into the underground river, knowing his friend would leap to his rescue.

In some sense, then, both boys were true to their pact: Tom was unwilling to live if Doug died from a blood disease; Doug leapt into the underground stream to keep Tom from drowning alone. Their story has kept both boys alive in Missouri legend.

Freddy's Story 1: Quarry

Janet Master's low laugh followed me out the door of her father's office, a very pleasant sound, I noted: "Hoo-hoo, ho-ho, hee-hee, haaaaah." Now that's a cheerful person, I thought. And having had my head opened up by stone dislodged from a motel wall only a few hours earlier, I appreciated good cheer.

I had never taken to this Stony Court job anyway. Stripping away a perfectly good rock facade to create some new look didn't make sense to me. And whoever had put this facing on a few decades ago, probably a local craftsman, had done a great job. This was a look appropriate to the region and to the famous highway I'd grown up along, Route 66.

At least in Missouri, I felt, America's Highway showed travelers the country's heartland--the great city of St. Louis and vibrant small towns, high hills and low river bottoms, abundant wildlife and honest folk. So it was crazy to trade native limestone for factory made siding.

Of course, I wasn't in charge of the Stony Court or the Sill Rock Company, and I followed orders. But a little distraction from an uninspiring project was welcome, especially when it came in the form of an attractive girl.

Janet Masters was more attractive to me than Helen Street, though many would have felt the other way. Helen was a woman, a little older than me, I guess, who was with a business group staying at Stony Court.

"You're not saving that old rock," she'd asserted a week or so earlier, as I stacked pieces loosened from the facade. I gave her a brief introduction to the craft of Ozark Giraffe, which didn't seem to impress her in the least. Since then, however, she always spoke to me as she came and went from the motel.

But it's funny to think that a playmate of my childhood, Janet Masters, had been so close for those three weeks I'd been working in Fairfield. I hadn't seen her after those days when I stayed with Uncle Jack and Aunt Mary.

The Potters had been kind enough to keep me for the few months after my family cme back from Illinois, when we were all a bit at loose ends. Once my parents finished repairs on the old farmhouse my dad had purchased near Lebanon, I joined them and grew up in the country.

My dad had tried to make a go at business in Chicago, but he never liked city life. The old farm looked promising as a site for the rock and gravel operation he'd wanted to start up since his war days as an Army engineer.

While I'd passed by Fairfield on Route 66 several times growing up, I don't think I'd come into town until this motel "restoration" job. On this project I rode back to Lebanon every evening with my dad, as that was cheaper than staying overnight.

My chance meeting with Janet wouldn't lead to anything, I was pretty sure. This was just an interesting coincidence connected to my current job. We had only another week at Stony Court, and then

134

I knew I'd follow the family business on to the next contract, even though I was less and less happy in my work.

Sill Rock Company had become quite successful, growing with the postwar economy by digging limestone out of the rolling hills of south central Missouri. That land is sparsely populated, and back then no one proposed limits to how big or how ugly you could make the holes left behind by your operation. All that mattered was having rock for roads like Route 66, for buildings on the expanding college campuses, and for homes to house the growing babyboomer population.

We also took some jobs involving stone removal, like the Stony Court project. Old man Bachmann knew the facade was worth something, and we paid him to let us remove it and then sell it to a builder at another site.

I, however, felt we were digging the foundation out from under ourselves. Sure, there's plenty of rock in 'them thar hills,' but I began to dislike the deeper and deeper pits we had excavated on our land, the shrinking hills that had once offered children from neighboring farms a great place to play. I hoped to stay in the family business no longer than a few more years, looking around discreetly for another use for my skills.

My dad wanted me to concentrate on making little rocks out of big ones, but I was looking to go in the other direction. I had developed a good sense about how to break rock into desired shapes, but I could also construct things from stone efficiently-- rock walls, terraces, facing. Any construction

135

projects I undertook, though, had to be outside the regular business.

I felt the greatest regret for the changes we were making in the Missouri landscape when I climbed High Hill, a favorite childhood getaway spot. Just beyond the border of our property to the north, it offered views that had been, when I was younger, inspiring. Now I could appreciate most of that beauty only in memory, somewhat like those farmers whose land had disappeared under the Lake of the Ozarks, which wasn't that far from us.

On one side of High Hill was a small spring, set back on a deep terrace up against a limestone cliff. I used to sit on some rocks there, listening to the water tumbling from a small pool in a miniature waterfall headed for the valley. The stream below was lost almost immediately in oak, hickory, and cedar.

Now, however, I could see a series of swampy pools connected by the exposed old creek passing open quarry pits and mounds of earth moved to get to the rock beneath. Gravel roads wound across the land to the county road by which we carried our product to customers. Also on view from my lookout point were a number of rusting metal equipment sheds, a few discarded machines, unpainted wooden storage bins--far from a pretty picture.

Of course, it all meant prosperity for my family, and for a number of years after I finished high school, I shared in the wealth--a Ford pickup of my own, plenty of money for beer, any kind of hunting or fishing gear I wanted. Lately, though, the enterprise was losing its appeal for me.

I'd always loved the lookout point on High Hill, both for the view and for the sense that it was anchored deeply to the earth. Most people don't know this, but Missouri contains the oldest mountain rock in the United States. The Ozarks are not as high as the Rockies or even the Appalachians, of course, but that's because they've been worn down more in their greater age.

So up there on the terrace, I had my feet on ancient ground, the foundation, in some ways, of the land itself. I think my love of rock--in buildings, walkways, basements, walls--comes from this feeling that so much can be held up by it. And it was becoming harder and harder to watch rock disappear from my home place, to see a beautiful stretch of Missouri being eaten away bit by bit.

This view wasn't exactly shared by my current circle of friends. I had taken my last girlfriend, Mary Lou Harrison, up High Hill one Sunday afternoon in the spring, thinking she might share my concern about this erosion of nature's beauty.

"It's so bright out here, Freddy," she said energetically on the climb up. "I mean the sunshine and all, with those flowers on the trees." The slopes were dotted with redbud and dogwood.

"The view above isn't what it used to be," I warned as I climbed behind her. She was a peppy girl, a lot of fun on dates, but maybe not the brightest person I'd ever met.

"It's weird I've never been up here," Mary Lou bubbled. She lived in town, where her parents ran a dry-cleaning store and she worked as a clerk. "How high is this?"

137

"I don't know exactly, just high enough to put us above most everything else. It makes you think, up

there." I was preparing to talk about my departure from the gravel making business.

She giggled, looking back over her shoulder. "You know what we can do?"

"No, what?"

"Have a peeing contest. You look for a spot where your pee will fall the farthest, and then I'll see if I can beat you."

After my visit to the doctor's office, I wondered about Janet Masters' love life. I assumed she'd gone or was going to college, and few girls of that generation came away from higher education unmarried. So she was probably already dating or engaged or even married and a mother.

Still, I thought, I ought at least to ask.

Bobby's Story 1: Flow

I have to confess I was immediately drawn to my lost, young well-finder when I found him puzzling around Great Uncle Bill's yard. It wasn't only that I felt sorry for him, working so hard with his maps and his tools and his questions to pinpoint the well's location. I guess I also appreciated his earnestness, even in confusion.

I didn't have much earnestness about my own tasks at that time, even though I had performed well in college and in law school. While I hadn't yet passed the Missouri bar, I had every encouragement from my law professors that this item of professional accreditation would come easily enough. It's just that I didn't know exactly what I wanted to do with it or where.

Lost Spring was a dying town, as the younger generation wasn't enthusiastic about the hard life of grazing livestock on mountainsides or sandbagging creeks to save crops in the bottoms. The big timber companies owned most of the land, and they brought in their own staff for big seasonal operations. Local young people wanted to get off the farm and on to Popular Bluff or Springfield, even St. Louis or Kansas City.

I, however, liked the quiet life I'd grown up with, focused on the land, family, and church. But there wasn't much legal business with the dwindling local population, most of whom distrusted law, banks, and the government. And what there was in the way of work was pretty much taken up by Duncan Fuller and Frank Chapman. Their fathers had set up rival practices here more than a quarter of a century ago.

My water-witching was still an enjoyable hobby, something I liked being called on to do for family and friends in the western parts of Arkansas County. But I had always refused money for my services, not wanting to face one unhappy customer even if a dozen had been satisfied. I'd known I had the gift since I was very young, probably before puberty.

Everybody thinks I know where water is, but that's not quite right: I know more often where it's going. My divining rod and I respond to underground flow. Where current slows and I feel water pooling, that's where I say drill. Over the years. I've been right far more often than wrong.

I knew where Louis Clark was going also, that first night I slept with him at the Ozark Motel. He wasn't going to become a geologist or an engineer or a corporate bureaucrat. He hadn't figured it out yet, but he wanted something entirely different in his professional life.

I could also tell he had a girl back home who wasn't holding him. He was going there for the weekends, but his eye had been roving all summer. And it had found me.

"I'll be coming to Lost Spring again next week," he told me for the second or third time that warm August evening, which I mark as a pivotal turning point in my journey through life. "There are more wells to find, you know."

"I might see you," I offered. "I'm keeping my parents' place while I study for the bar."

"That's in Lost Spring?"

"Well, nearby. But I could probably see you in Arkansas, too, if you'd like."

"Sure! I'll be at the Ozark again."

I held in check the smile that wanted to spread across my face at his eagerness. I hadn't thought he was a virgin when I took him into the room, but now I understood his excitement. He was so grateful!

I didn't know then if he would be more than brief summer entertainment for me, but I decided to enjoy myself as long as I could. If this proved only a pleasant break from cramming, that was OK. I was in the process of readjusting to life in the country, anyway, and diversions were just fine.

Seven years in St. Louis had made city life stale to me, but I hadn't been deeply dissatisfied until the last year or so. Then I kept finding that there was just so much building, so much traffic, so much frantic insistence on getting something more than everyone else had. The men in law school were mindlessly cutthroat; the women were cruelly ambitious.

At the end of my time at St. Louis University came Jackson Steyne, who completed my disenchantment. I should have known where he was going, and perhaps in my heart I did. But when we got there together, I balked. I made the break final before graduation. Now, hiding out deep in my native Ozarks, I was taking a wait-and-see philosophy about my own future.

Things had certainly seemed clearer when I was ten years younger, a talented and attractive high schooler from a strong family celebrating my first great success as a diviner.

My parents were traveling that summer, in South America, as I recall, and I was left in charge of the house. Our neighbors, the Andersons, had kindly invited me to a family cookout after church. Just as everyone on the big front porch was settling down from the last round of homemade pie topped with hand-churned ice cream, the alarm went out: little Beth Thompson, age nine, was missing. One of the children, all of whom had been eating on two picnic tables out under the oak tree, said she hadn't touched her pie. When someone asked where she was, no one knew.

"Oh, she's fallen into the water, I'm sure," her mother cried immediately, jumping up and wringing her hands in her cloth napkin. The creek, swift and full from recent thundershowers, was no more than forty yards down the hill, bordered by high brush.

"Who saw her last?" asked her father. He looked around a bit wildly. "Are you sure she's not in the house?"

"I just came from inside; no one's there," said the little girl's aunt, Mrs. Martin, from up Persimmon Tree Road. We all scanned the yard, realizing we saw everyone but Beth.

"Let's go," Mr. Anderson said. "I'll head east, down to where the creek pools by the cow barn. You," he pointed to his brother, whose farm adjoined his property. "You go west, as far as the bridge." That was where the drive up to the house crossed over the creek. In the short time she'd been out of sight, Beth probably wouldn't have gone farther.

"Beth! Beh-eh-eth!" called her mother, already running in the direction her husband had proposed to go.

She's not there, I thought to myself with sudden conviction. And then I called out, "Wait! She's not in the creek."

"What do you mean, Bobby Green?" said Mrs. Anderson, one of the few able to stay calm.

"She's . . . she's not at that water. Look by the well."

The Andersons' old, hand-dug well was out back between the house and the barn. I jumped down from the porch and sprinted around the house. I didn't mean their new well, which was enclosed in a small cinder block structure.

A lone dairy cow, a small flock of chickens, and a dozen cats and kittens shared space in and around the barn. They scattered as I came racing toward the well.

Perched on the rim of the old stone structure sat Beth, absentmindedly looking down into the darkness. She had managed to push aside one of the planks that covered the opening.

How did I know where Beth was? Well, most others thought at first it was a lucky guess, but later changed their minds as I began to witch for water. I wondered if it might have been some form of unconscious communication, Beth contacting me through telepathy, but I had not heard voices inside my head. Later, after more occurrences like this one, I came to understand my relationship to water: even when I couldn't see it or touch it or smell it, I knew where it was. Or where it was going.

Even that's not quite all, I think now. I knew there was water in the creek and in the well. I understood where it was all moving, how it connected, how it flowed. But I also knew where Beth Thompson was going that summer Sunday afternoon. She did not want to see moving water. She wanted the still surface at the bottom of the well. She was throwing a penny in, she later told us, making a wish.

I made a wish myself that day. I asked to let my discovering Beth not be an accident. It wasn't. But that has also meant my life hasn't always been easy. It wasn't easy, for instance, when I first learned about my great aunt's will.

Freddy's Story II:
Cool Pool

The week after my visit to her father's office, I realized that there might be a place I could offer to take Janet Masters on a date of sorts. If she wasn't interested in this outing, I'd know pretty quickly that we didn't have much in common, beyond having lived in the same neighborhood for a few months when we were small children. So I called from the pay phone on the wall outside the office of Stony Court.

"Dr. Masters' office," she answered. "How may I help you?"

"Janet Masters?"

There was a pause. Then, "Yes. Who's calling, please?"

"It's the boy with blood on his head, Freddy Sill. The other day?"

"Oh, yes, of course. Are you having trouble? I don't think it's time for the stitches to come out. Isn't that Friday?" I could hear her rustling the pages of the appointment book.

"Right. Actually, I was calling you, not the doc. I wondered if you ever go out to Cool Pool?"

"Cool Pool? My family used to, before the Fairfield Pool."

"Yeah, I've heard it's bigger, more modern. But there's something at Cool's I might show you. We can swim if you like, and they also have that picnic area. We could just get something to eat." There was a silence, so I went on: "I've only got another week or so on the Fairfield job, and I thought it might be fun to see what we can remember about life fifteen years ago. Formative years, you know."

"I'm going to be in the library Saturday morning, reading up on a . . . a problem. What time did you mean?"

"Saturday afternoon would be good for me."

"I could go then. There's another spot down Route 66 a ways I might want to stop at."

"Sure. Pick you up around 3:00?"

"OK. I guess you know where I live." And she gave one of her low laughs.

"There's only one other thing."

"Yes?"

"Do you mind riding in a pickup?"

Another chuckle. "You'll find out Saturday."

So it was on, a date with the doctor's daughter. I liked that low chuckle of hers more than Helen Street's sharp laugh. I'd heard that Stony Court customer sharing Mr. Bachmann's low opinion of local politics as he escorted her out to the company car one day recently. She barked assent to some sneering comment he was making about the town mayor, Mr. Paterson.

There must have been half a dozen big shots in Miss Street's team, and I deduced that they'd been in the area for nearly a week. All out-of-towners, they seemed to be hatching some commercial scheme. Perhaps a light industry was looking to put a plant here; it might be that a growing bank wanted to build a Fairfield branch; maybe they were trying to get a tax deal for some new Route 66 related establishment.

Fairfield was a growing community, and it wasn't far from an expanding Fort Leonard Wood. There might well be opportunity here for me as well. I'd done work besides chiseling old Ozark Giraffe loose from the Stony Court Motel.

Cool Pool (named, believe it or not, after the man credited with first building it, Samuel Cool) was a primitive swimming facility about fifteen miles west of town, made by simply damming a spring-fed creek. There was a natural stone floor in one turn of the creek, and Cool had built up the banks around the pool with loose rock walls. It wasn't watertight, but the creek's flow kept the basin full behind a crude dam.

The spot was really not much more sophisticated than a natural swimming hole, the spot of deep water along a creek or small river Missouri kids have found on their own since, I'm sure, people first came here. Our state's great for such waterways, which were the Indians' highways. They're also the sites of this era's fishing, swimming, and boating recreation. They establish boundaries, provide water for town and farm, become sources for hydroelectric power.

Cool's began loosing business, of course, when the new Fairfield municipal pool opened three summers ago. And the owners (the original Cool's sons-in-law, Herbert Taylor and Jack Stephens) realized they would have to make changes to keep the business afloat (so to speak).

Travelers and local residents were now courted by roadside advertising, radio commercials, and discount coupons in the *Fairfield Mirror*. Folks were encouraged to take a break from the heat and enjoy afternoons swimming or sitting at picnic tables and desk chairs around the pool. They could buy food at a concession stand, including burgers cooked on an outside brick charcoal grill. Fun for kids and adults!

My (paid!) contribution to this improvement project had been sprucing up the rock wall of the pool facing the highway with Ozark Giraffe. It wasn't a big job, but I'd done it on my own time and received some convincing compliments. That small project was one of the hints that I might be able to go off on my own.

I also had, in the back of my mind, yet one more reason for visiting Cool Pool: I hoped to exorcise an old ghost.

You see, my uncle had taken me, along with his own children, to Cool Pool one Sunday afternoon during those weeks I stayed in his house. It was summer and hot, and he made a specific effort to find special activities for me, the family guest.

Like my cousin Ernie, I had not yet learned to swim, but there was a good sized shallow end at Cool's. Where the creek entered its natural rock basin, the water was only about a foot deep. And I remember splashing happily about where I could feel the current rushing over the low wall at the pool's edge.

At some point, though, my uncle got the idea that I would enjoy floating about the deep end in a little yellow inner tube shaped to resemble a duck. It had a head at one end, a tail at the other. Resting in the center, with arms braced over the rim, my legs were free to kick in the water beneath.

Who wouldn't have thought this was a great thing? A non-swimmer could go anywhere in the pool the swimmers could. And, I wasn't just left on my own in this inflated duck. Uncle Bob kept a close watch on his nephew, recognizing the possibility, even though unlikely, that I might slip through the center in a moment of exuberant play.

I, however, didn't like this arrangement. It's not that I feared drowning, sliding into the water. I'd already learned how to put my head under with eyes shut and nose clamped between thumb and forefinger. I couldn't tread water or dog paddle yet, but I was comfortable in water that wasn't over my head.

What bothered me was that I didn't like my feet not touching bottom. I felt that I was disconnected somehow, pulled apart from some touchstone. It would have been the same, I believe, in a backyard swing if it'd been set too high to kick off at the base of the arc. I am a person, I suppose, who wants his feet on the ground. I understood this instinctively then, and, as I grew older, I confirmed a tendency to fear breaking the connection between me and the earth.

It took some more growing up before I fully understood the phobia, of course. In fact, I must have been moving toward this discovery when I decided to invite Janet to Cool Pool.

I'm sure, that is, that this anxiety came upon me because I had been separated from my parents. My relatives were great to take me in; I remember playing happily around the new neighborhood; there was no uncontrollable crying or wetting the bed at the Potters' house. My parents were careful to come by, perhaps once a week, telling me about how much they'd done on the house, asking me if I needed anything, checking with my mother's sister about me.

I can even recall insisting that I liked it in this neat neighborhood full of kids, that it was great to have a temporary "brother" and "sister" (as I am an only child). But still, I felt disconnected, adrift, not quite grounded.

Fifteen years later, more or less, I thought it might be a good idea to see if I'd outgrown that childhood anxiety by revisiting Cool's Pool.

Bobby's Story II: River's Bend

My great aunt was the only daughter of a wealthy New York woman, widowed at a fairly young age. I had been her favorite ever since my aunt first came to visit in Arkansas County, perhaps twenty years ago. Just a month after being graduated from law school, I learned that I was mentioned in her will. This was an event that surprised my parents and made me wonder if some important new avenue might be opening up for me.

I didn't have any idea if the property she'd left me was really worth anything, but I appeared to have stumbled into a person who could at least show it to me, Louis the well-finder, Louis the (former) virgin.

Aunt Betsy's nephew, a big time banker in Boston not yet thirty, had, in the same letter that told me of my inheritance, offered a modest sum for this parcel. He'd explained that the property had little potential for farming or development. It was near Fairfield, a sizable town, but had no access by a major road. Much of the land was rocky, he claimed, the timber thin, the soil barren. But it was over 100 acres, and I did wonder at his price being so awfully low.

When I told them about the inheritance on the phone, my parents, traveling in Europe, thought I should just take the money. They pointed out I had never been interested in living any place except Lost

151

Spring. The money I was offered could buy a nice piece of property in our remote county, which I might hold as a long term investment or build on myself in later years.

I agreed that this inheritance could establish me on a nice parcel of land, but I still figured I'd have payments to make, bills to pay. That meant employment, almost inevitably away from Lost Spring, where my only calling was as unpaid water-witch.

My gift of divining, by the way, missed one current in Louis' talk with me during our second meeting.

"So, um, you want to go eat or something?" he asked on the phone late one afternoon as I puzzled over these questions of my future. At the beginning of his second week working the area, I had left a note at the motel desk for him with our number.

"Eating sounds good. But you don't know where we should go, do you, where the locals eat?"

"That's true. But I'm going out with a local, aren't I?"

"OK. So, I say you need to visit River's Bend and eat some catfish."

River's Bend, on the outskirts of Arkansas, featured country fried food, especially catfish caught in local streams and eaten on the same day they were pulled out of the water. Nowadays, most places serve farm grown catfish, easing the fears of those who worry about bottom feeders.

Now, it's true that fish who take to the deepest water can get into all sorts of crud that sinks to the gravel under the main current. But in those days, in those remote areas, fast moving, unpolluted streams made native catfish fine eating. And, again, since I was trying this wellfinder out for a time, I figured I'd better see how he did with deep fried fillets, strong cole slaw, and biscuits made with lard.

"You want me to pick you up?" Louis asked.

"No, I'll drive. Even though you're the map wizard, it would take too long for me to tell you how to find my place. Or River's Bend."

River's Bend was a favorite place for me because of the water. True, anyone could see where that water was and where it was going. You didn't need to be a diviner to find a rushing current breaking over rocks one hundred yards above the turn in the river where the low wooden building sat on the bank. A witching rod would not have been required to locate water actually flowing beneath the floor of the front porch and main dining area, which were built on stilts. Still, I always felt especially at ease in this setting and with the friends and neighbors I always found gathered here.

I volunteered to drive Louis in part because I was pretty sure he wanted to end up at his motel again, and this would give me control of my own destiny, a chance to say no, if that's what I decided. After we'd had dinner, though, I realized he had had designs on my destiny I had failed to pick up on. I had been thinking sex, but he was more serious.

"I took a look west of Fairfield this weekend," he told me while we waited for our orders to arrive.

"Oh? Not the place I'm interested in?"

"It probably is. I checked records at the courthouse, looking for any large parcels changing hands out that way."

I watched him drink some of his Coke, straighten the silverware at his place. He didn't seem nervous in this noisy place, pretty well full for a weeknight. River's Bend had another room they opened up for Friday and Saturday. But his composure could have come from lack of attention to his surroundings rather than confidence about fitting in.

"And you found a sale?" I continued.

"One in progress, nearly 150 acres, not so far from town. I walked around out there a bit. It's nice."

The basket of french fries arrived and plates with fish, cole slaw, the richest biscuits I've ever eaten. He looked at it, I thought, without emotion.

"I understand it's not worth much," I explained. "Poor access, rocky."

"Well, right, there's no road in right now. But it isn't that far from Route 66, and I didn't see any reason something couldn't be developed. There are plenty of survey flags all around. Someone seems to be thinking of the property as a potential site for some project."

"Survey flags? Well, I guess that would make sense--the thing's going into an estate. Still, I wouldn't think they'd need to survey until the heir--that's me--decides what she wants to do with it. If I just keep it as is, there's no need for a survey."

"Hmm." Louis was listening but also eating. He seemed satisfied if not excited by everything in front of him. I also had to conclude that he was searching for a way to ask me back to the motel. He'd lost his virginity, but I doubted if he had learned the sophisticated art of seduction over the last weekend.

"I'm not sure they didn't lay out a roadway," he went on. "Now that I think about it, that's how I found my way in. There were parallel markers running south from the highway across an adjoining field and then into the main parcel."

"That's interesting. Of course, it's been assumed that I don't want the land, that I'll sell. But I've said nothing about what I really plan to do. I haven't signed anything."

"Oh," he said, looking up suddenly. He wiped his mouth carefully with the paper napkin, folded it neatly and placed it beside his plate. I figured he was ready to move on to what was really in his mind, a roll in the hay with the country girl. But he surprised me by talking about someone else.

"I saw this girl out there," he said. "Actually someone from my high school. I didn't know her, though, back then. Janet Masters. Anyway, she said it's all going to be an amusement park. Sounds like another Disneyland."

"Whoa! Maybe this isn't my land. It must be some other piece of property."

"Maybe so. But it should be easy to check. Do you have any official documentation, something from the estate executor?"

"Yes, of course. But not with me."

"I'm sure I can tell from that. I've got that quadrangle in my car. I can show you where I was on Saturday."

"I'll come in tomorrow night and bring it with me."

"Good. You know, you could also come see it this coming weekend. You could even ride up with me."

"Oh, that's asking a lot of you, and I'm keeping my parents place while they're away. They have their dogs, things to take care of. Maybe I can just drive up Saturday, come back the same day."

"Well, OK. But . . . " He hesitated.

"Yes?"

"Bobby," he said, and the seriousness of his tone finally caught my attention. "Bobby, I want you to meet my mother."

Freddy's Story III:
Bearbaiting

I was ready to go swimming at Cool's, or do all the other things one might pursue at this primitive recreational facility: spread a towel on the hillside and watch the other swimmers; have a picnic at one of the wooden tables behind the pool; play pinball in the waiting area in front of the snack counter. But I was most interested in talking with Janet and seeing what kind of person she'd become besides someone with a deep, long laugh. I found she had grown up into a young woman about ready to wrestle a bear.

I made this discovery while we were taking a hike through the woods before we even got to Cool's. She'd heard about some kind of theme park to be built west of Fairfield, and she wanted to check out the most probable site for such an enterprise.

"I could see some things going in here," she said, as we climbed out of my pickup truck to inspect the area. "I mean, if we need more houses, we could keep the basic look of the place the same. You don't have to cut down all the trees, and there's space to keep parts of it as small neighborhood parks."

"This is pretty country, Ozark foothills," I agreed. "I sure wouldn't let Sill Rock Company in here!"

"You mean they'd dig it all up for the rock?"

"That's right. In a year you wouldn't recognize the place."

157

We were parked on the side of Route 66, several miles outside of Fairfield. Two ruts in the dirt started across a field, but, twenty yards from the highway shoulder, everything was grown over with wild grasses. Across that field were woods sloping down, probably to a creek, with another hill rising behind that.

"But that's your family business, isn't it? What else do you do?"

"It's the family business, but I'm thinking of moving out on my own. Doing some different things."

"Hmm. I'm not sure I've ever seen these woods from this side." She paused at a little rise where the grass filled in the ruts. "You can hike in from my neighborhood, you know, the Circle."

"I remember going down to the tracks. And some empty lots across from my uncle's house."

"No, this is out the other way. We might have been too little then to go roaming that far from home. I probably didn't start coming out here until five or six years after you moved away."

"Ah, how quickly they forget!" I joked, and then kind of wished I hadn't. She seemed embarrassed about not having remembered me when I'd come into her dad's office with a cut forehead.

"I try not to forget . . . things. In fact, I'm studying history at college."

"Where do you go?"

While we were talking, she started out across the field, following the remains of a path that once had probably been a road for farm machinery or for logging. There were survey markers here at regular intervals.

"Columbia. The university. I want to be a teacher."

"Teaching's good. But you're also telling me you're an outdoor person. Looks like you might be good at recess!" She was striking out so purposely into the woods on the far side of the field, like an energetic teacher leading students on a field trip, that I had to pick up my pace to stay even with her.

"I do like being outside. This is probably my favorite place to be in the whole world. Especially by this spring over . . . " She gestured vaguely off to the south, "Over that way."

Janet was wearing cutoff jeans and a T-shirt decorated with St. Louis Cardinal symbols--the bird, a ball and bat, Bush Stadium. Her shoes were a kind of desert boot, good for hiking. And shoulder length hair spread out from the bottom of a basketball cap. I compared her casual outfit with Helen Street's business attire. The Stony Court patron wore dark short skirts and expensive blouses, stockings and high heels, hair cut close to her head.

"So you're worried all this will be changed--huge parking lots, amusement rides, fast food, and carnival games. The creeks will go underground or be channeled for boat rides, the rocks made part of fantasy lands or hauled away to make room for plastic ones along some artificial jungle safari."

"Oh, it's even worse than that. They want to call this place Hillbillyville. A travesty!"

"A place for city people to come make fun of country folk? I know what you mean."

159

I'd never had much to do with city dwellers. I'd spent my life with rural neighbors, small-town friends from school, and local business customers of Sill Rock Company. Whenever anyone from Springfield or Jefferson City commissioned us, my dad did the talking. But I'd seen enough movies and television shows to know the stereotype of the country bumpkin--the citizens of Green Acres so obviously less sophisticated than Eva Gabor and Eddie Albert.

"Even at school, if you're not from St. Louis or Kansas City, you're a hick," she said with a fierceness I hadn't expected. "And now they're going to hire kids from Fairfield and the county to act like dumb rustics to earn money for fat cats living back East or in California."

Her face had gotten red, and she practically spit out these last few words. This was when I realized Janet Masters was a girl who'd wrestle a bear if it were necessary!

Somehow I'd never been particularly bothered myself by the phenomenon of hillbilly baiting. The few times I'd confronted that kind of snobbery I'd kind of enjoyed myself. It had happened, in fact, about ten days earlier outside the Stony Court.

Another of Helen Street's business associates was Mr. Briefcase. Well, I didn't know his real name, of course, but I never saw him without that all-important black leather satchel in his hand. He didn't know my name either, or even see me working around the place until he needed some help one day.

We'd backed a truck up to the building to remove a load of facade and left it idling temporarily in front of a row of parked cars. Mr. Briefcase's company car was blocked, and he wanted to get out.

"You there, Jethro or whatever, get that truck out of my way."

"Me?" I was the only one close at that moment, restacking the stone in the truck bed. I assumed he was talking to me, but I didn't like the way he asked. So I figured could play dumber than he wanted me to be.

"Yeah, you, sonny boy. Move that damn thing. I've got to be at the bank in five minutes."

"Well now," I said slowly, with my best southern Missouri drawl. "Weh-hell nah-how, I'm not let to drive that there truck. I ain't got me a license. They say my Ma shouldn't had married my Dad 'cause they was brother and sister. But, hey now, the key's in it. You can go on ahead and move it yourself."

I'd suspected that Mr. Briefcase couldn't drive a straight shift, let alone a duece-and-half. And I was right.

"You go get someone to move that truck. Where's your boss?"

"I cain't ask my boss nothing, mister. He's always telling me to shut up. That truck don't need to be moved but a few feet anyway, looks to me. Go on and you drive it."

"Where is this boss of yours. I'll get him myself."

"Let me see now if I can rightly remember . . . Was it in the office? No, no, I think he went over't The DC for coffee." I'd found that locals pronounced the name of this diner "Thee Dee See," so I doubted if he even knew what I was talking about.

I was beginning to take some pleasure in this conversation when he said a word I didn't think could be found in his briefcase and stormed off. I could sympathize with Janet about his type and resent a plan to market the hillbilly stereotype.

When she and I had spread our towels in the shade halfway up the hill south of Cool's Pool, I looked forward to presenting myself as the true Ozark boy, not a character from some television series. The wall I'd faced with Ozark limestone, which was nicely in view from that perch, was just the thing to show her who I really was.

Bobby's Story III: Turtleback

Louis did not press me to come back to the Ozark Motel with him after we had eaten, but I was drawn on by his intense need to keep things in order. At River's Bend Louis made sure his plates and silverware remained neatly arranged. The Survey car parked outside was uncluttered. I found the motel room looking as if the maid had just finished her work.

There was, I concluded, a current of anxiety under the surface order that Louis maintained so intently. It had come out during dinner when he told a sad tale about an old lady whose well he'd found in Peculiar, Missouri. I didn't see why what troubled him shouldn't be brought out into the open. So I threw back the covers and wrestled him onto the sheets.

It also took no time at all for a bubbling inner excitement to break into view: he was finding sex even more fun than his years of adolescent imagining had suggested.

"Oh my gosh, oh my gosh!" he cried out when I'd rolled him over on the bed and pulled myself back from the tip of his excitement.

"Don't hurry," I whispered into one ear, retreating with my hips from his hips. I'd thought a condom would dull the sensation and allow him to last longer than the first time, though I wondered if he could hold himself in check even while putting it on.

He froze instantly when I asked him not to hurry, but all he could say was still, "Oh my gosh, oh my gosh!" His eyes were wide, he held his breath, and the concentration visible on his face as he tried to keep himself under control was positively touching.

"For just a minute," I urged, "think of something else. Imagine . . . I don't know . . . that you're looking for a well. Driving down a gravel road, past an old white farmhouse, a little spotted dog barks . . . "

"Oh my gosh, oh my gosh!"

Perhaps it was in part because he was so embarrassed at being unable to delay his release that my sympathy for this boy swelled again. I agreed to come see him and his mother in Fairfield on Saturday.

I'd been getting a bit stir crazy at home anyway, studying Missouri law eight to ten hours a day. My parents' house was isolated, set deep in 150 acres of timber off an unpaved county road. Though I was at home in those woods, I sometimes wanted company while Mom and Dad were enjoying their latest stay in an Italian villa.

If I went to Fairfield Saturday I could also look at the land I had inherited. It wouldn't be where I wanted to live, I was pretty sure. But I ought at least to look the property over.

I'd heard about the kind of place I'd like to own earlier that summer, a farm called Turtleback. There are a number of places like it in the Ozarks, isolated ridges surrounded by moving water. But this was even more cut off from the rest of the world than most. A problem for the future, of course, was how I would earn a living at a place like that, so far from civilization. But right now I indulged in the fantasy of life on Turtleback.

The Cutt River winds through south central Missouri, a modest stream famous for its clear water and its driving force. It loops back on itself many times, traveling thirty miles sometimes to advance five as a crow flies on its way to the White River down in Arkansas.

Often one of those big loops winds around a high mountain ridge, making that hill a peninsula reaching out into a ribbon-like stretch of water. With steep sides to the ridge above the rushing river, there's only one way into that piece of land--the neck of the peninsula.

Turtleback was just over a hundred acres of woods and about thirty open acres in a long thin shape three hundred feet above the river. There was one climbing, winding gravel road up to the top of the ridge and a hunting cabin at the far end of the ridge. It sounded like just the place for me. Well, for me and one other special person.

This Ozark retreat was quite a bit different from Fairfield Gardens, where Louis had grown up. He lived in a tiny house in a tight neighborhood. The houses were bunched up next to each other on little crescent drives.

Mrs. Clark explained how they'd been fortunate to keep their two-bedroom frame house after her husband's death. He had been a jeweler with, apparently, a poor sense of time, at least in terms of keeping up with payments. I noticed an unusual number of timepieces among the sparse furnishings of Mrs. Clark's home, including an odd coocoo clock in the living room. I tried to avoid too many of their questions about my parents' larger house and greater means, but I had already revealed to Louis the fact that I was inheriting property near Fairfield.

Still, the three of us had a very pleasant lunch together. I'd gotten into town by 11:00, called him, and he'd directed me to their house. We went through the usual formalities, questions about family, school, plans for the future.

Louis had announced my visit as business, Uncle Carter's well having brought us together and his expertise a happy coincidence for me. In all our pleasant conversation, however, I picked up on an unspoken concern on Mrs. Clark's part. Something out of the ordinary was troubling her.

I've always been good at this, hearing what people are not saying as well as what they say. It's another aspect of my divining, I suppose. (Of course, with Jackson Steyne I'd turned off my gift, burying the simple fact that all he wanted from me was his own pleasure.)

I realized what Mrs. Clark was not saying as I was carrying dishes into the kitchen for her. Louis had gone to his room to get the right maps for our afternoon drive to see this property I believed I was inheriting.

"Louis is such a good student," she'd said when he was out of earshot. I think she didn't want to embarrass him in front of me with these expressions of maternal pride. "He works so hard."

"I could see he was a serious worker when he explained his job at the Survey to me."

"Yes, sometimes on Sundays, before he goes out for the week, he reads up on the area where he'll be working. There are books at the Survey that describe the terrain. They list facts about the water table, the drainage, the things that will help him find where people have put down their wells."

"I guess you become an expert in a job like that. I'd like the fact that it's outdoors, not an office job."

"He wants an office job, though, eventually. He plans to work for a big organization, something permanent. But he still has school to finish, two more years."

"The large companies do provide security. You can start at a low level, work your way up, stay with the same institution your entire life."

This wasn't what I wanted myself, to be swallowed up in one giant team of lawyers and accountants. My ideal had always been a solo practice or the small family firm. Unfortunately, there just wasn't room for even one more lawyer in Lost Spring.

"Did you know that Louis has just broken up with a girl he's dated for over three years, Linda Forrester?"

"No. He hasn't said anything about that." I had sensed it, though, in his manner with me. He had felt guilty when we kissed outside the Ozark Motel, and afterwards, but not for what we were doing. It was that he had not been doing it with another girl!

"Ever since his father died, he's kept a lot to himself," his mother continued, shaking her head and wiping her hands on her apron. "He thinks . . . he thinks he's not supposed to need anyone. Anyone but me, of course."

"He thinks a lot of you, Mrs. Clark. When I told him I had to come this way, on business, he insisted on our meeting."

"Yes, I know. He wants me to hear what he's doing. He counts on me to always . . . be here, for him."

And this is when I realized that this quiet, small woman already knew she was dying. And she wanted her son settled before that end came.

Freddy's Story IV:
Crossroads

"See that wall down there, making the edge of the pool on this side?" I asked Janet at Cool's Pool.

"Sure, the rock wall. It's pretty."

We were sitting on towels spread out on the hillside rising from one side of the pool.

"I'm glad to hear you say that," I responded. "I did the facing."

"Oh! Now I see, it's like the walls of Stony Court. Odd shapes of stone all pieced together. It's a gigantic, vertical jigsaw puzzle."

"It's called Ozark Giraffe, and it's a style developed in this area. I've learned some on my own, but one of my dad's foremen is an old craftsman, and he's helped me a lot."

"I like it. How do you get all the pieces to fit together? They're such different sizes and shapes." She was looking more closely now at my wall, which was about fifty to sixty feet long and ranged three to four feet in height.

"You get better as you work at it, seeing what piece will go where. But you also break the rock with certain ideas about the shape of the parts you'll get. Of course, it takes experience to predict how stones will split and come together. The old guys say there's a pattern waiting to be discovered in any collection of stones."

"Those slab-rock buildings look something like cobblestone houses, now that I think about it. I've seen pictures of them in history books. England, I think, has a lot of them."

"I don't know about that. Most of the time around here the rock is just the outside, embedded in cement. But some people do put pebbles into a cement mixture and pour it all into wooden forms that can make strong walls, a whole building. I guess that's like cobblestone, now that you mention it."

"Maybe early emigrants from the Old World introduced the technique here?"

"Well, the nice thing is, for Ozark Giraffe, you use what's right under your feet. Missouri's famous for this limestone. It's everywhere, and it can be shaped easily by someone who knows what he's doing."

"I'd never really thought about that. I've seen those buildings, like Stony Court, all my life, but never wondered about where their walls come from. A Show-me architecture, huh?"

I was feeling good about this conversation. I'd shown myself as a true citizen of the area, not a cartoon caricature who might fit in the background of some Hillbillyville. I noticed, though, that Janet had started looking around Cool's Pool as if she hoped to see something--or someone--else.

"You can also strengthen old wooden buildings with this rock facing," I continued. "That's what I'm trying to learn from Mr. Jensen right now. I'd like to specialize in fixing up older places with Ozark

Giraffe, stabilizing and grounding the structure. I think it could be its own business."

"That's a good idea. I'd rather see old places fixed up than torn down and replaced by new things that aren't as pretty. Is that what's happening with Stony Court?"

Here Janet seemed to be giving me just the right opportunity to show myself as the savior of Ozark values. I could be the hardy pragmatist who relies on what nature provides for a task at hand, not importing foreign material and techniques. Yet I'd show that I understood beauty too, balancing shape, texture, and function. I was a little disconcerted, though, when she craned her neck to look over the concession stand in one direction and back past the highway in the other. What was she searching for?

"Humph!" I said. "Mr. Bachmann is going with an asbestos siding that I don't think looks good. Still, it will probably last a long time. It's a tough material."

"Surely not as tough as rock!"

"Right. And what Bachmann will put up there doesn't occur in nature, not on its own. It's the result of a refining process. Fibers are extracted from rock, then reconstituted to create siding or other material like ceiling tiles."

Janet stood up and exclaimed, "I bet that's it!"

"What?" I jumped up too, surprised that my attack on asbestos had inspired such an explosion.

"This is just the kind of place where it probably happened!"

Oh, gosh! Had she experienced something terrible here in the past, some scarring incident? Or did she somehow know that I'd been traumatized at Cool's years ago when, riding in my uncle's yellow rubber duck, I'd felt disconnected from any foundation?

"What?" I said again.

"This is where the wagons broke the trail."

"Come again?"

"Well, look," she said, pointing excitedly. "The river comes through here northwest to southeast, right? See those hills? It's winding around them, there. And then it crosses this level stretch where we are, turns past those trees, disappears on its way . . . I guess it will make it eventually to the Gasconade."

"OK, I see that." We had walked farther up the hill to see all this. "But I don't see the point . . . ?"

"The Indians traveled up and down waterways. Rivers created a network that connected different groups, the tribe as a whole."

"And Cool's was probably a watering place for game, for deer especially." I began to understand more of what she was saying. "So Indians could come up the river hunting."

"Right. But the white man, coming west, was working in a different system. I mean, eventually it would be the railroad carrying manufactured goods to the frontier, food back to the cities. But even before that, they were headed west looking for land to settle, new places to start over again."

"And you're saying this is a crossroads, cowboys and Indians in the same place but going different directions?"

"Yeah. And a turning point for history too. The story of this region was once governed by creeks and rivers, natural paths beside which people walked. Or they rode up and down them in their canoes. Then came modern man, industrial man. And his roads were for hauling cargo, not hunting and fishing."

"I guess this could be one of those paths west, then--the Santa Fe Trail?"

"Well, both the Santa Fe and the Oregon Trails began in Independence. They crossed Kansas and then headed south- or northwest. But this might have been a way for some pioneers journeying to, maybe, Oklahoma and Texas."

It made sense to me, though why she had such interest in these things still wasn't clear. I also thought about even earlier times, before humans roamed the area. The rock at the bottom of Cool's had been worn smooth by water, ancient paths to and from it padded by the feet of animals, some now perhaps extinct. There was a history before history.

"Well," I offered, "we could be standing at a significant place, I guess. Something important in the past."

"Yeah, but I'm thinking about now too. Not exactly here, but where we were earlier."

"The future site of Hillbillyville?"

"Future site only if we let it become one! Some Boston-New York-Philadelphia fat cats want to transform Phipps County, send us all in a different direction. Down the road to Tinsel Town."

"Well, they do have the money, don't they? And the land."

"I still say it's not too late. What we need to do is organize, plan some protests, get public opinion behind us."

I almost said, "We?" After all, "we" were only on a first date. But I realized I'd like to have another date with this budding activist, so maybe there could be a "we." This date at Cool's could turn out to be a turning point for the two of us.

The intersection of my story with Janet Master's had made me wonder where I had been headed on my own. Now it could be that I was changing direction to go down the road this savior of the woods was already traveling. It just could be.

What I didn't realize then, of course, was that more than two of us were coming together at this place and time. And, though we would find a road to travel in common, it wasn't going to be an easy journey for any of us.

Bobby's Story IV: Aunt Miriam

"So, you want to tell me about your family?" Louis asked as we pulled out of his driveway on the way to tour my recently inherited property.

"My family?"

"Well, you've met all the Clarks there are. I'm the only son of a widowed mother who was an only child who lost her parents early in life."

"Ah. I'm an only child too, though my parents are still living. They're . . . uh . . . traveling right now."

I could see he was a careful driver, regularly checking his speed, glancing at the rearview mirror, scanning the traffic ahead. He'd folded the maps so that the relevant portions were visible and mounted them with a clamp to the dashboard.

"Your folks away on business?"

"No, pleasure. My dad's semiretired. He, um, invested in a friend's business, years ago, that did really well."

"That's nice. So your mom doesn't work?"

"No, they married when they were still teenagers, before Dad went into the Army, in fact. He was in Europe."

"I see. And where does this inheritance come from? I mean, if I'm not being too nosy."

We'd come to Highway 00, the road I'd driven up on from Lost Spring. It continued north across Route 66, went over the Osage River into Jefferson City, then crossed the Missouri River.

"Oh, no. You're not prying. It's my great aunt Miriam. She was a New Yorker. Well, she lived there but used to visit us in Lost Spring."

"Those are two different worlds!" Louis seemed quite taken with this idea. From his mother's remarks I concluded he saw in this confirmation that one could move from one to the other. I knew he wanted to rise to a secure place in that urban world.

"Yes, but her people came from Missouri. Near Fairfield, as I remember, but I don't have that family history completely straight in my mind. Aunt Miriam had a row with her mother when she was younger, I think, and the two didn't talk for decades."

"That's sad. If you've got family, you should stick to them."

There was the slightest click in his throat when he said this. He might have been thinking about his father.

"Well, when Aunt Miriam's mother died, she left her the income from property, but not the right to sell that property. Her history is probably even more interesting than Aunt Miriam's."

We had turned west on Route 66, America's famous highway. I'd been close to it in St. Louis while I was in school, but I didn't particularly think of myself as connected to the Mother Road, having grown up so much further south.

"Tell me about your . . . grand great aunt? Your property's not much further out this way."

"OK. Her life was a series of radical changes. She spent her childhood on the Missouri frontier; then her family pulled up stakes and went back East. Whatever they were doing--farming, trapping, trading--must have failed."

"This was a hundred years or so ago? The time of the Civil War?"

"I guess so, before that, probably. Anyway, in Cleveland, I think it was, both of her parents died in a smallpox epidemic. Then she was taken up by one of her mother's old friends and her husband, a childless couple in New York City."

"Ah, the center of the known universe!"

"And certainly the home of America's nouveau riche, people like the Rockefellers and the Carnegies. And Lucy's new, adoptive parents had plenty, so she went from rags to riches."

"OK. Here's where your land is, or at least where I think it must be."

We had crossed the highway median and pulled off the lane into the beginnings of a dirt road headed towards some woods. It wasn't much more than a couple of ruts in the grass, but Louis had space to park. We got out and surveyed the terrain. He oriented himself with the topographical maps he'd carried.

"I thought it was off the highway?" I said.

"It is. This field isn't part of the property, but it starts not too far into the trees there." He pointed. "And it spreads out east and west, parallel to Route

177

66. If you could buy a right-of-way through here, the area could be developed. Homes, I guess, or an industrial site, if anyone was interested. The soil's pretty poor."

"Let's walk on it and see what we see."

I could already see red survey flags tacked on tree trunks and dangling from bushes. None of the trees was very large here, and a lot of rock showed in the ground. This was poor soil, probably cleared when the first white settlers came through and then farmed out by successive plantings of the same crops. I could tell where creeks drained rainfall from the hillsides and created a sizable stream that crossed Route 66 off to our right.

"Since you're a lawyer," said Louis as we walked into the woods, "I guess you can't have much use for this. You'll be a town dweller, working in some tall office building, part of the city skyline."

"Maybe. I can't see that I'm drawn to it, though."

"Why not? Gosh, that's security. Big business, the corporation. You get your niche, and nothing's going to come along to change things."

I recalled what I'd come to believe about his mother. She was dying and anxious about how her son would survive a second great loss in his young life.

"I don't know. It seems to me change comes no matter where you are." I also remembered Jackson Steyne, my one-time city lover. He had sure as heck altered my life.

"You can take deliberate steps," said Louis with characteristic intensity. "You take deliberate steps to insulate yourself, build up a structure of protection. You look around, study the lay of the land, identify the safest place to be. It's sort of like drilling a well: put it down where the water's always going to be. You can find that place."

"Well, my great aunt's mother, Lucy Something--I don't remember her last name--she had to face upheaval after upheaval. Her parent's business failure, then their deaths. She was adopted by wealthy people, but then she married a man who pulled the rug out from under her dreams."

"Oh?"

"Yeah, a speculator. He gambled away her first fortune in stocks and investment schemes. About all they had left when he drank himself to death was their daughter, my Aunt Miriam."

"Did her adoptive parents take her back?"

"No, they were gone by that time too, and their fortune went to a nephew, the sole remaining male relative. What saved Lucy was a second marriage, to another New York tycoon. He was rich, but ancient. He died within a few years of their marriage, and, according to Aunt Miriam, Lucy made sure of her inheritance this time."

"She controlled it herself?"

"That's right. And she made safe investments, including land in Missouri that had belonged to her ancestors. That's how this property comes to me, I guess. From Lucy to Miriam to me."

"Why was Lucy buying land way out here when she lived back East?"

"Well, apparently she had fond memories of her childhood around here. She used to travel back to the area . . . when would that be? I guess the 1920s. Aunt Miriam told me about some place that had been important to her, where Lucy's mother kept a garden. And either she bought that very land or some much like it."

"So maybe there's something special about this property we're walking on. You just don't know its place in history yet."

"There's at least one spring on this land," I observed, scanning the rise and fall of low hills. "There's too much water otherwise." Louis studied the map, probably looking for a spring.

I thought about it all for a moment, then said, "You know, I need to actually see Aunt Miriam's will. I wonder if there's not some sort of mission here I'm supposed to undertake."

Freddy's Story V:
the Ground Floor

"I'm going to show you the spring," Janet said as we pulled out of Cool's and started back on Route 66 toward Fairfield.

"The spring?"

"Remember I said you can come to that place where they're going to build Hillbillyville from our neighborhood, the Circle?"

"Yes."

"Well, there's a spring down at the base of a cliff there, prettiest place I've ever known. And, well, I'd like to show it to you."

"You're going to enlist me in your people's campaign to save the wilderness, aren't you!" I laughed.

"Maybe. I sure am going to need all the help I can get. Mrs. Anderson's says I'm crazy even to think about it."

"Mrs. Anderson?"

"Oh, she's this centenarian who comes to Dad's office all the time, a real Fairfield character."

"Ah, but someone who's been around long enough to know how things work, who's behind what project and why."

"That's right. I like her because she's unconventional. But she knows the history of our town practically from the beginning."

"And she thinks it's too late to stop this theme park?"

"She tried to convince me that everybody believes it will be good for the town--jobs, tourists. It will put Fairfield on the map."

It would put Fairfield on the map, I realized. And, I have to admit, as we drove east on Route 66 I thought about that development in a selfish way. After all, there would be plenty of construction in such an enterprise. And I was in the construction business. Sill Rock Company would probably get some big contracts here: carrying in rock, removing rock, shifting rock around as the site was prepared. The family business could really prosper.

But this might also be the perfect opportunity for me to branch off on my own, putting Ozark Giraffe on any number of buildings. What better style for Hillbillyville, I reasoned, than this native craft already visible in so many structures of the area? The situation might even allow me to slide out of Dad's business gradually. It wouldn't be a rebellion but a natural application of my individual ability in a related direction. There could be two Sill Rock Companies, both enterprises to be proud of.

This is, I believed, how careers were made: you get in on the ground floor of some important new venture. It's not so much that you're better than anyone else. Your timing is just luckier.

After all, humans share certain elemental abilities in approximately equal degrees: analyzing, relating,

182

constructing. So it's who's standing at the right place, the base, when something big gets started.

My own father had found this out in wartime, though he was on the other end of the process that I was interested in. Trained in explosives, he had blown up enemy fortifications throughout France and Germany. But the same principle applied: if you knew where to place the bomb, you could bring any structure down.

I think he was actually pretty good at destruction, though he always told me everyone he'd worked with in the Army could do what he did.

"Just study the foundation," he'd say. "There will be a weak point, on which everything rests, directly or indirectly. You pull out that bottom rung, and . . . ker-bloom! It falls into a hole." "Ker-bloom" was one of his favorite words.

I admired my father. The challenges of his generation had been huge: surviving the Great Depression, fighting World War II, building a stronger nation under the threat of nuclear conflict with the Soviet Union. He never complained about the obstacles he'd faced and overcome.

When he talked about his wartime experiences, he acknowledged only the technical problems and successes. There had to be losses, men killed and wounded. But he never mentioned them, ending most stories with a satisfying "Ker-bloom!" Only much later in my life did I wonder why he never heard from or contacted old Army buddies.

I had assumed, of course, I'd do my time in the Army also, but a congenital eye defect had disqualified me from enlisting. I had a single tiny blind spot in one eye, and it showed up on the vision test. I couldn't even qualify for national guard duty.

I suspect I went into the family rock business as a way of fulfilling a sense of duty, trying to emulate my father. If I couldn't be a soldier like he was, I'd follow his footsteps in my career, at least up to a point.

Now, however, as I've said, I was beginning to think I might like to do something a little bit different, get involved in building, in addition to or rather than collapsing. I was a long way from those beatniks and protesters I saw on TV. No better than hoodlums most of them, I thought. But I did believe our generation might make some changes in the American way of life. Rather than always battling something, maybe we could unify opposing forces.

"We can walk in here," Janet said. She had explained that she ordinarily hiked from her house back to the spring, but my pickup, she figured, could take the gravel road south of the Circle to within a hundred yards of the spot. The road ended in a small clearing at the base of a ridge marked by sharp granite outcrops. So we followed a path across that ridge, passed the ruins of a log farmhouse, and wound down the far side to the bubbling pool.

"What's it called?" I asked Janet.

"It doesn't have a name, so far as I know. Not very many people know about it. It's tucked back in here, and I don't think anyone's been in that house up there since the last century."

It was a beautiful spot, I gave that to her. The trees were taller and fuller than what you find in most parts around here. Our woods were usually more scrub trees than forest, since early settlers had cleared large tracts for farming and this was all second growth. Here ancient walnuts and hickories towered above us, rising parallel to the chalky cliff that encircled the spring. The clear water gave off a sharp, fresh smell.

"I can see this place in Hillbillyville," I suggested. "They'll channel it to a mock still surrounded by moonshiners."

"Barefoot I'm sure, and smoking corncob pipes."

"Worrying about revenuers, the 'gov'ment.'"

"All to the laughter of touring Californians," Janet concluded. "They'll build a stage around it, put in seats for the audience, and play bad country music over loud speakers."

Her vision of the future was not pretty, though it wasn't as bad as what had happened in my lifetime to the scene below High Hill. From my ledge vantage point, beside a much littler spring than this, I'd seen the landscape of the Sill family farm transformed from a scene of natural beauty to something akin to a war zone.

We'd been careful to hide much of this from the view of folks who drove down the county road that came by our farm. And the farm itself was out of the way of major traffic. But from two-thirds up High Hill, I could see gravel pits, drainage pools, dead trees whose roots had been crushed by heavy equipment.

I had a certain respect for old Samuel Cool of Cool's Pool. He'd done the least he had to in making a natural swimming hole into a modest local business. Taylor and Stephens, the current owners who'd hired me to spruce up the pool's wall, had done the same. They understood what Ozark Giraffe was and sought out someone skilled in that art. Mr. Jensen had kindly suggested me for the job of uniting man-made wall and God-created landscape in this project.

I wondered who'd be happy to see Janet's spring lose its Ozark character and become a Hollywood set piece. At once I thought of that smart business woman Helen Street, well tailored patroness of Stony Court. No softness beneath that professional appearance! She was all work, no play, and let's make money.

"Janet," I said. "We're going to need some help in this operation." Then I pointed through the trees. "But right now I want to know who that is coming down the trail."

Bobby's Story V: *Confluence*

"Let's go further in," I said to Louis. "I might as well see all there is to this place so I'll know what decision to make about my inheritance."

"There's some kind of building here," said Louis, pointing to a black square on the map. "Probably a farm house."

"OK," I said with sudden inspiration. "Take me to that house's well!"

"The state Geological Survey at your service, Ma'am."

Louis had marked the property's boundaries with a red pencil, so I could see its irregular shape. I'm sure a psychologist would be interested in what different people saw in that outline--a cloud, a sleeping dog, the shadow of some bird of prey. Whatever someone envisioned would reveal her view of the world.

Aunt Miriam's view of life had turned melancholy in her later years. When she first came to visit our family, she'd brought presents and sunshine, especially to me. She wasn't technically my aunt, of course, but an aunt a few times removed.

My father had an older half-brother, who had grown up in another state, and they had never been close. That half-brother was Miriam's second husband's cousin. No one could figure out exactly what that meant our relationship to Betsy was, but we always called her "aunt."

My father had met her through his Army buddy, Gene Chapman, whose business had made us all wealthy. At a stockholders' meeting in New York he was introduced to Mrs. Miriam Branch, another important investor. They were amused to discover a family connection, and it led to one of those polite invitations Midwesterners always make to Easterners: "Stop by whenever you're out our way." We all assume no New Yorkers will take the offer seriously, as they think of our region as a backwater. But Miriam had unexpectedly done so the following summer.

"That must be the house," Louis said as we came out into a clearing on the top of a ridge. The "house" was more a cement foundation with crumbling log walls surrounding a pile of rotted lumber. In the center were remains of wooden shingles, carved logs, caked mud that had been used to seal gaps in the walls.

"The letter I have about the property doesn't admit to any structures," I explained, pulling out the papers I'd received about the estate.

"Nobody's lived here for decades," Louis asserted. "Probably not since the last century. I suspect this was somebody's farm that failed a long time ago."

"The area on the south would have made a good garden," I observed. "And who knows how much of the land was once cleared for crops?"

"The way the ground is leveled out this way, this house may have once been much larger. You'd have to dig to find the original foundation."

"I'm still not sure why Aunt Miriam left it to me. I kind of feel she wanted me to do something with it. But she may just have wanted to include me in her will somehow."

I scanned the documents in front of me, most of which were legalese putting forth the boundaries, the acreage, how much timber and how much field. Down at the bottom I noted the one restriction: the inheritee must agree to assume permanent residency on the property. I suspected such a provision might be circumvented, but I'm sure that's one reason for my initial feeling that I would prefer a sound cash offer. Now I asked myself if this condition also pointed to my aunt's notion that I was to undertake more than ownership of this particular piece of real estate.

Aunt Miriam had been impressed with my divining early on, not that she ever wanted a well dug. She felt my gift would lead me to happiness, something she claimed had eluded her in the end.

I recalled one summer visit while I was in college, a warm afternoon with the threat of thunderstorms in the air. On the patio out back watching my father barbecue chicken, I asked Aunt Miriam what it was like to live in the most important city in the world.

"I'm sorry to tell you, Roberta." She always called me by my full name, insisting that only boys were called "Bobby." "Roberta, I never did learn how it was done."

"What do you mean?"

"You've heard of Central Park?"

"Of course, it's in the center of Manhattan, right?"

"Right. You see, I grew up next to Central Park, in a tasteful and very expensive apartment. And I always thought of the Park as my center, the base of the known universe."

"I can understand that, the city's so important to the whole country."

"Yes. And being at the center I thought I could see the forces that blow individuals this way and that, like the discarded paper swept down the street by the wind. So I'd control my own destiny, avoid the pitfalls and find the pots of gold."

"Do you mean money, fortune?"

"No, Roberta, I was born with those. No, I mean true friends. People to grow old with."

"You've never married, have you?"

I realize now this was a pretty tactless question, as women in her generation who did not marry were "spinsters," an unhappy and unsuccessful lot. But as I've said, Aunt Miriam was especially tolerant of me.

"No, though I have rejected a number of matrimonial offers." She smiled, a wistful, contemplative look settling on her face. "But I could read all those signs correctly."

"Signs?"

"Oh, you know, who wanted my money, who knew he could move up in society, who might really have cared for me but for . . . circumstances. Those things I knew. But that wasn't enough. I needed reference to some more solid foundation, something

190

even deeper and older than the streets of New York."

She paused again, looking west to where the clouds were getting darker. She said, "Can you tell when it's going to rain?"

There was rumbling in distance, but in the Ozarks thunder travels many miles through mountains and valleys in unpredictable courses. Rain could be imminent or occurring many miles from where you stand.

"Well, I can watch the clouds, smell the air when it's close."

"I mean the way you can find water. Using your . . . what do you term it? . . . your dowsing rod, your powers as water-witch."

"That's not the same thing. I find water underground, where you would want to dig a well."

"What I'm referring to is quite similar, my dear. There are many things I could do in the city-- organize charity balls, assist at the hospital, attend dinners and parties. These are tasks I learned growing up as the daughter of an eccentric but very wealthy socialite."

"Your mother who was born here in Missouri, who had such fond memories of her childhood?"

"Yes, she did. Of course, I came into her life quite late, when she had survived two husbands and the loss of two fortunes. She was used to having her own way when I began to question the course she had selected for me. It was not an easy time."

Aunt Miriam's reference to difficult things in the past seemed underscored by the storm's moving closer. There was little time between the flashes of lighting and the crashes of thunder.

"It's time to go inside," I said, getting up.

"You see, Roberta, you do have more than one gift! You can find water underground and you can feel rain coming from the sky. When it involves choosing someone to be happy with, or finding a life that has meaning, I'm a person who never learned to come in out of the rain." We got into the kitchen just before the storm broke.

Louis broke my reverie of Aunt Miriam's lament by observing, "There's a path going down behind the house. Let's see where it goes."

That path, of course, led to the destiny Aunt Miriam felt had eluded her, but which, it turns out, was patiently waiting for me.

Freddy's Story VI:
Appointments

Janet introduced me to Louis, who'd gone to her high school. And he introduced us both to Bobby, the lawyer. Pretty quickly, we four assumed we'd solved a major problem: we were two couples whose coincidental coming together would prevent the corruption of a scenic landmark.

When Janet discovered Bobby had a legitimate claim to the property we were standing on, she went into one of those long, deep laughs of hers. It was a release of tension that had been building since Brad Whitaker pressured her to get married earlier that summer, just before Lucy Rivers Johns' bottle popped to the surface of this very spring.

Louis and I felt a similar exhilaration, but for slightly different reasons. Neither of us had the courage to declare our feelings yet, but we hoped to impress these girls. So supporting their plan to rescue a doomed wilderness was an obvious course.

Oh, and how powerful is the innocence of youth! This idealistic vision brushed aside known barriers and dismissed any unseen obstacles that lay before us. But we four kids had been so little tested in our coming of age during a relatively peaceful era that it would have been naive to gamble on our efforts.

Hillbillyville, it turned out, had the momentum of months--no, years--of preparation, as well as the support of people who were used to success. The deal was easily 90 per cent complete at the time Janet was reading Lucy's letter in a bottle. On our side, only Bobby the attorney could claim any kind of professional standing, and she, like Janet and Louis, was still a student in one sense (trying to pass the bar). And I was just a skilled worker employed in my own family's small business.

Now, it's true that Route 66 Spring could be said to come into being with the summer afternoon arrival of this foursome at an abandoned farm west of Fairfield along America's Highway. But as we got to know each other better, we only slowly learned how our separate interests and abilities might work to one purpose.

Consider, for instance, just one individual we didn't at first recognize as standing in our way: Helen Street. I'd had clues that this assertive businesswoman staying at Stony Court was a player in the Hillbillyville syndicate, but I'd paid no attention to what a number of hints might have shown a more experienced observer.

Miss Street's accent said she wasn't from this area, though I couldn't place her specifically. My knowledge of regional speech came from what I heard in movies and early television shows--hardly enough to distinguish Philadelphia from New Jersey or Los Angeles from San Francisco. I'm the kind of person anyway who hears the underlying patterns people have in common more than subtle variations on the surface.

Wherever she was from, I believed Helen Street's lack of interest in local affairs suggested she would leave Fairfield the minute she finished the business she had come for. She was here to take what she wanted and then return to her chosen field of operation, certainly a major urban center.

But she did, as I've said, lower herself occasionally to speak with me on the grounds of Stony Court. On that day I was injured, in fact, she had actually offered her help.

Earlier, I had been on a break, chugging a Coke as I leaned against one of our company pickups in the parking lot, when she walked past. Miss Street had just gotten out of a car driven by Mr. Briefcase, a man I didn't like and who didn't like me. She greeted me in a friendly manner.

"Sill Rock Company," she noted, reading the printing on my work shirt. "Your company around here?"

"We're two counties west, not far from Fort Leonard Wood. We work the south-central Missouri area."

"Um-hm. I'll catch up with you in a minute, Martin," she said to Mr. Briefcase. "When the call to Chicago goes through, I'll be ready with the paperwork."

I don't think Martin distinguished me from the sledge hammers and crowbars that were being used to loosen Ozark Giraffe from motel walls. But, then again, I didn't see him as any more alive than the expensive suit he wore or the leather briefcase he carried. He couldn't pass by, however, without revealing his resentment of my material reality.

"Why do we have to put up with this?" He waved a hand at the rock, the dust, the equipment,

195

me. "I told Stan he should have put us up at the Banner." The Banner was the most expensive hotel in Fairfield, out on Route 66.

Miss Street ignored him, and he went into the office. Then she said to me, "Has all your work here been outside?" She pointed to the exterior walls.

"Yeah. Our job is to get the rock out of here, and there's none inside. It's take it down, load it up, carry it away."

"And you're just dumping it somewhere, making gravel or something."

"Oh no, it's valuable facing. We've got a builder down near Lebanon who wants it."

"Well, it doesn't appeal to me. But the insides of these units at least are reasonably attractive." She pointed to what I assume was her room, dangling a motel key with its large wooden tag in the same hand she pointed with. "I've enjoyed my . . . my nights here." In that pause she gave me an odd look.

"Well, we don't even spend nights in town on this job," I said. "It's cheaper to drive back and forth from home. Of course, we leave some of the trucks and most of the equipment here." I gestured out to the side parking area where Mr. Bachmann had set aside space for us to store our machinery.

"Sometimes I could use a little recreation here," Miss Street continued with a chuckle. "Not much to do in Fairfield!"

I didn't know what to say to this. There was certainly more to do here than on the Sills family farm, especially now that the view from High Hill was so diminished. She went on. "Maybe you could stay late one night and tell me what you would do around this town. For fun. Or I could show you . . . "

She trailed off, glancing toward the office. Right then I wasn't having much fun back home, since I'd broken off with Mary Lou Harrison some weeks earlier. Mary Lou was the girlfriend who wanted to have a peeing contest, and I wasn't going to use her to show Helen Street the richness of life in small-town Missouri.

"I guess we get back to basics around here--family suppers, mending and fixing things around the house, not much going out."

"You, um, you don't have a girlfriend, some sweet young thing ready to climb up in your big pickup truck?"

"Well, not right now I don't."

"Let's go, Freddy," a voice called. My boss was walking over from our office trailer on the side parking lot. "Bachmann wants us to pick up the pace, get the north wing done today."

"We have to be careful there, Mr. Jensen. That stone's so well set up we have to go slow to save it."

197

"Yeah, I know that and you know that. But this guy don't give a damn about the stone. Excuse the language, ma'am. It's just, 'get it the hell out and gone.'"

I excused myself to Miss Street and went back to work. But that pressure from Bachmann is what led to my accident. Mr. Jensen and I hurried the dismantling of a delicate section, and one loose piece came down on my head.

It turned out that, at the moment the rock got away from us, Helen Street was coming back out of her room with Mr. Briefcase, I guess having finished her transaction with Chicago. And, seeing the blood, she recommended I go just down the street to Dr. Masters' office, "two blocks, other side of the road."

As you know, the injury was superficial, and I was back at work in less than an hour. But one question did begin to take vague shape in the back of my mind that afternoon. It never made it to the forefront of my consciousness. If it had, I might have been more prepared for what Janet and I discovered a few weeks after we linked up with Bobby Green and Louis Clark.

That question was this: why did Helen Street, who had taken so little interest in the life of this little town, know immediately the name of a local doctor and where his office was located?

Bobby's Story VI: Ants

I couldn't tell at first if they were a couple, this doctor's daughter and the rock carver. Janet had explained how she was showing Freddy her favorite place of childhood, which I took as a sign of some intimacy. And Freddy talked about how he'd been exploring with her the idea of leaving his family's business and starting out on his own. Again, this suggested closeness.

Of course, wondering about them was probably an indirect way of bringing up for consideration the same question about Louis and me: were we romantically involved?

True, we had already slept together twice, and I'd come to his home to meet his mother. But I'd thought of our two meetings in Lost Spring as recreational for me, a change of pace in a slow summer of study. And driving up to Fairfield that first time was at least part business, the matter of my inheritance. Louis, I suspected, had taken this much more seriously than I.

Perhaps this connection with the serious well-finder was more than idle pleasure for me after all. Maybe some things in my inner self were coming out, forcing a confrontation in my conscious mind. This happens, of course, more often then most of us want to admit: concerns buried in our formative years make their way into the light at certain moments of adulthood, sometimes creating havoc in the careful plans we've laid out for ourselves. Perhaps some of us develop sufficient self-confidence to let such fierce beasts out of their caves deliberately, but my guess is more of us are taken by surprise.

I think now I was coming closer than I realized during this time to acknowledging a long felt desire. When we four young persons made a semicircle around our spring, watching and listening to the steady bubbling of cool water rising up from underground and then flowing around us and down the valley, I felt the powers of liberation and self-discovery.

Louis, of course, was the slowest to see what his past had done to him. His response to his father's death had been to lock up any hopes for happiness in an obsession with order. His mother worried that nothing would free him from the habit of trying to control everything. Freddy, on the other hand, was the most open of any of us about what frustrated him.

"You know," Janet said as we were ready to leave the spring. "You know, there was terrible locust destruction through the Mississippi Valley in the 1870s."

"Hm," we all said. This didn't seem to connect to anything we'd been talking about--Hillbillyville, local businesses, our plans for the future.

"Yeah," she went on. "Cicada nymphs live in the ground and feed on roots. They come out and eat everything they can find."

"OK," one of us agreed.

"So, that's what locust swarms do--strip plants of their leaves, create whole fields of stalks and dirt."

"Oh," Freddy said. "You're thinking that's what will happen here, just about a hundred years later."

"But the locusts are people," I chimed in. "The builders of theme parks."

"Exactly. And the thing about locusts is number. There are so many that no single person can stop them."

"It's like 'Lenninger and the Ants'," said Louis with sudden excitement. "'Lenninger' or 'Mennager'--I can't remember."

"What do you mean?" I asked.

"I heard it on the radio." He and his mom used to listen to the radio a lot in the evenings when he was younger. "It's a play set somewhere in the tropics. A bunch of farmers are worried about their crops at first. There's talk of armies of red ants, millions of them, eating everything in their path."

"Oh, I've heard that!" says Janet. "I think it's 'Leinegan vs. the Ants.' It was on *Suspense*."

Suspense, one of the last great radio dramas, aired in the evenings on CBS through the 1950s. The introduction featured a famous drawn out pronouncement that each episode was a tale "well calculated . . . to keep you in . . . . *Suspense*!"

"So this guy, Leinegan, is eaten by ants?" asked Freddy.

"Right," Louis went on. "There are just so darned many of them. Their bites are not deadly, but still somewhat poisonous, so each one weakens the victim. And thousands eventually kill whatever they're biting. They swarm up over, say, a rabbit even while it's running, bring it down. Then they take a dog, a deer, it doesn't matter. And Leinegan-- or whatever his name is, the hero--he has to . . . "

"He has to set up a fire line, doesn't he?" interrupts Janet. "With oil in a ditch or something."

"That's right," agrees Louis. "The ditch is there, but he has to run to the oil tank, open it to fill the ditch, then set fire to it. It will stop the ants on one side of the house."

"I think the idea is to turn the ants in a different direction," says Janet. "You can't stop them, but they can march off away from your home. Or maybe the ditch goes all the way around the house. I can't remember."

Louis picks up the story. "Well, we can hear Leinegan's thoughts as he runs toward the oil tank. He's put on high boots and gloves and whatever he can, but the ants are climbing up on him as he runs. He's swatting and saying 'Got to get to the barn . . . before they reach my face . . . my eyes.'"

"You can hear him breathing, huffing and puffing," agrees Janet excitedly. "It's a scary deal."

"As I remember," Louis concludes, "he doesn't make it. They get inside his clothes and he's hitting at them, trying to squash them, but they blind him and he falls. It's the end of the show."

"I remember it differently," says Janet quietly. "He might fall, but just as he reaches the tank and releases the oil. Somehow it gets set on fire. Everyone is saved."

"Well," Freddy concludes. "Whatever happens on *Suspense*, we're going to have to turn these ants, these Hillbillyville people, in another direction if we want to preserve this place. Get them to buy land in another county, another state."

"Well, that should be easy," I laugh, and we all recognize we don't have the resources for this sort of maneuver. But I realize I am the key here, the heir to Janet's spring and the land around it. I'm also, in a sense, the brains of the outfit, in that I've been trained in the law. I should be able to find out why this project has gotten so far along without securing the property.

It makes me think back to why I went to law school in the first place, aside from the fact that I was encouraged by my English and political science professors. They predicted I would do well on the entrance tests, and they knew I enjoyed being a student. But I wouldn't have taken their advice if I had already been searching for something my father missed.

You see, his family had farmed land around Lost Spring for four generations, beginning with a Horace Green who came by foot from Tennessee in Daniel Boone's time. They never had money in the bank but always food on the table--food grown and harvested on beautiful Ozark land. We owned about 300 acres.

When Dad gave Gene Chapman half the pay he'd earned in the war, he thought he was just helping a buddy who'd gone through hell with him. He had no idea what to do when he was suddenly wealthier than anyone in the county. That was ten years ago, I guess, when I was a happy farm girl who was also good at school.

I had come along late in my parents' married life, by the way, a surprise but a welcome one to this very close couple.

When Chapman's company, an electronics firm, hit it big with government contracts, my parents built a spacious new home. They leased out acreage to other farmers and began traveling in this country and abroad. But lately their lives seemed to involve wandering more than journeying. Though he didn't quite know it, Dad was missing the necessities of work, the daily and seasonal rhythms that had given meaning to his world for nearly seventy years. I figured this out while I was in college, though I never found a way to tell him, concerned daughter to loving father.

I went to law school in part, then, because my folks could pay for any education I desired. But I was also stalling until I could identify a focus for my own life's work. And now, right here before me lay Route 66 Spring bubbling with meaning.

Freddy's Story VII:
Powers that Be

Janet was as much sad and hurt as surprised by what Sophie Anderson told her about Hillbillyville.

The two pairs of us--Janet and I, Bobby and Louis--had been agreed on a general plan ever since leaving the spring that Saturday afternoon. Janet was going to ask her friend who raised laboratory animals about theme park investors. This ancient Fairfield resident should know who was involved in the project.

I had to head back to the Sill farm that and other evenings, but, since our work at Stony Court wasn't done, I'd be in town again every weekday. I was to see if I could learn anything about the planned theme park from Helen Street. Janet would meet me whenever she could for lunch at The DC, the little diner just a block from her dad's office.

Meanwhile, Bobby, back in Lost Spring, had formally notified her cousin that she was not ready to relinquish her inheritance at the price offered. Then she began researching the strength of the residency clause in her great aunt's will. If she didn't have the right books at her parents' place, she could call one of her professors at St. Louis University for help.

Louis had wondered who owned the small piece of land along Route 66 that could provide access to the property, and he said it might be wise to know about adjoining properties on all sides. His work for the state Survey had given him experience in ferreting out just this kind of information.

I'd like to say we were a team of trained agents, spreading out over the countryside to carry forward a well-orchestrated operation. But that would be more than a slight exaggeration. Still, the four of us, haltingly perhaps, were nonetheless homing in on a reasonable scheme.

"You won't believe it!" Janet said in a hushed voice as we sat one Wednesday on the last two stools at The DC. She was controlling her speech because she didn't want to be overheard. But I noted the anger in her words.

"Mrs. Anderson gave you the scoop?" I asked.

"Did she ever. It's a lot what we expected--the mayor, both bank presidents, most of the people who are anyone around here."

"They're not going to be happy to learn Bobby won't sell."

"Well, I'm sure they still think she will. They've got plenty of money, so my guess is they believe they can up the offer until she accepts. And there are some out-of-town investors, represented by that Street woman."

"They're in Chicago?"

"Most of them, but there's one from Boston. He's apparently in town too, but I wouldn't know him if I saw him."

"It's probably 'Mr. Briefcase.'" I explained who I meant by this. I hadn't told her of my exchanges with him around Stony Court, not seeing any need to increase her resentment of those who made fun of local residents.

"You know what's funny!" she went on. "At Mrs. Anderson's I felt I was inside Hillbillyville, or at least a model of it."

"With her animals?"

"Yeah. The mice, the rabbits, the hamsters--they were all little Ozarkians squealing for food and . . . and making messes on the newspaper at the bottom of their cages."

"Ugh!"

"And I thought about her house, how she'd changed it from the neat family home it must have been long ago. The yard in back is completely covered with little wooden and wire structures. I think there was once an old stone well near one corner, but I couldn't see anything for the fences that divide one kind of critter from another."

I could see how this seemed a preview of the future for her, the loss of her spring in a fantasy landscape. But it didn't fully account for the intensity of her look, the way she almost spit words at me. Well, not "at" me, because she had seemed genuinely glad to meet me, but in my presence.

The more Janet described the crowded zoo of Mrs. Anderson's, the covering over and concealing of the original house, the more I found I too wanted to get to the bottom of this entire Hillbillyville scheme. How had it all come to be, anyway? At times it seemed a deep mystery.

Even this lady herself, nearly 100 years old according to Janet, had a past obscured by her current actions. She had been around far longer than these people out to make some money. I wondered how she came to be in this house, for instance. When Louis learned of her, he called her, mysteriously, "another peculiar old Lady." Whatever that meant, I knew we'd have to dig to find all the sources of the current situation.

Working with Sill Rock Company, I'd learned that, when you dig with shovels and machines in Missouri, you go through layers of different rock. And generally you go back in the past when you do so, through sediment pressed down on earlier sediment. And you need to remember that our state's hills, mounds, and mountains were not pushed up to the surface by forces of upheaval. Instead, they are what's left after erosion, ancient structures standing where softer material has washed away over millions of years.

Interestingly, it's not always the case in northern Missouri that the deeper you go, the farther back in time you're traveling. In the Ice Ages glaciers carried giant boulders and other material from the north to the top of those areas, and some of that rock can be older than what's beneath.

What we'd come across with Hillbillyville was the surface of something that had been brewing for a few years, a plan to shape this community according to the ideas and needs of outsiders.

"So," I said to Janet. "So the thing to do still is make sure Bobby keeps the land. I guess she'll have to live there."

"Yes, but I'm not sure she'll want to do that. I wouldn't want to pick up myself and leave here to live somewhere else."

"Good point. But you never know. I'm thinking pretty seriously of moving from the farm to Fairfield."

"To start your own business?"

"That's right. Well, and to continue getting reacquainted with my childhood."

"I think . . . I think that's a good idea. I mean, I could maybe help you find a place to live around here. And show you the town, before it's transformed by Hillbillyville."

"Thanks. I'll take you up on that."

"You can be like Luther Taylor Johns."

"Who's that?"

"A pioneer of the last century. He built up the first successful iron works in this area. And he had a beautiful home, with a spring his daughter used to love."

"Just like your spring?"

"It might even be the very same spring. I tried to research that, but couldn't locate exactly where the Johns place was. The house didn't need to be right at the spring, though, because he had this Fountain he'd invented."

"Fountain?"

"Yeah, a gravity powered pump that pushes water uphill through a pipe."

"But gravity pulls things downhill."

"OK, I guess I need to show you a drawing. But it works. I read about it. You know, you might be like Luther Johns with your rock work."

"I don't think I can make rock flow uphill!" I laughed.

"No," she agreed smiling. "But you could build things up, from the ground. Your rock walls and your Ozark Giraffe facing could rise up from the land and create a good space for people to live. You could be Johns' spiritual heir."

"That doesn't sound so bad. I don't seem to want to inherit my father's business or his way of doing things. But what about you? You're going to teach history, not be in the medical profession like your folks."

She grimaced when I said this, and I wondered why.

"I don't think that's bad," I hastened to add.

"Oh, Freddy, I hope I'm Lucy Rivers Johns' spiritual daughter, because I don't want the same things as my parents." And then she said with the saddest look, "They're among the biggest local investors in Hillbillyville!"

Bobby's Story VII:
3-D Pictures

When the phone rang on a Thursday several weeks later, I assumed it was my parents, checking in from Italy about their scheduled return to the United States. But it wasn't.

By this time Louis had moved on in his survey work to counties south of St. Louis, searching for wells during the week and coming down to see me on Saturdays or Sundays. He was a courier of sorts for our anti-Hillbillyville group, but it was also clear he wanted to see me. I realized I wanted to see him too, more than I had expected. My only concern was his leaving his mother on these weekend getaways. I had not shaken my feeling that she suffered a terrible illness and was not telling Louis.

I stayed busy during the week myself, studying for the bar but also exchanging letters with Martin Flint, the distant cousin who conveyed the offers for the land west of Fairfield. As Janet had predicted, the price was increased several times, but Mr. Flint made no reference to who the buyer was or what that buyer intended for the property.

An additional piece of my inheritance also came by mail: a packet of letters written by Aunt Betsy's mother, forwarded by her attorney. It seemed an odd gift to me, until I read them. Then family history and my great aunt's will made a lot more sense.

Aunt Betsy's mother had become obsessed with establishing a private park in Missouri on the land where she had grown up. Though she'd had to leave it while still a girl, nothing from her later life in Ohio or New York had come close to inspiring the same fondness. Especially important to her was a beautiful flower garden her mother had developed with native plants, laid out in geometric patterns and punctuated with large stones carried by her father up from creek beds and down hillsides. She wanted to create a similar retreat for citizens of the future where the scenic quality of Ozark flora, fauna, and topography would be preserved.

This lady had come back to Missouri frequently in her later years, apparently wealthy enough to buy the land she wanted but unable to persuade the owners at that time to sell. There were also complications with the idea of a trust to maintain the park and questions about who it was designed to serve.

In her letters she tried to persuade Aunt Betsy, then a young woman, to take up the vision she herself had failed to fulfill. Betsy finally did buy the property, very near the end of her life. And she put a provision in her will: I had to live there and ensure that no changes to the site's natural beauty were allowed.

That beauty grew on Louis as he went back to roam about the land. He also met Janet and Freddy several times at the spring, the property's most compelling feature.

"It's funny," Louis told me at one point. "I've been seeking water for two summers now all across the state. With my maps and compass and altimeter, I've driven across the plains in the north of the state and climbed up and down hills in the southern half, never really looking at what I was passing."

"You mean you were just focused on the wells, finding them and entering the data for the record?"

"That's right. But we have such a beautiful state, its woods and ridges, every kind of creek, stream, river. At Janet's place, I finally stopped working and just looked."

"Well, I have a thing about water myself, especially natural water. It's kind of in my blood." I paused, then went on, "You know, Louis, something else might also be right in front of you without your truly appreciating it."

"Yeah?"

But I found I couldn't blurt out directly that he was taking his mother's health for granted. He remained closed off to things that might disrupt the future he had planned so carefully. Even I was a problem for him. He couldn't seem to do without me, but he'd also begun to realize I didn't want the same things he did.

Having initiated him sexually, I found he possessed an insatiable desire. We would have sex many times in the day or day-and-a-half he spent with me in Lost Spring. And we were everywhere: in my bed, on the porch, in the hayloft, down by the creek. He couldn't stop himself. And it turned out I didn't want to stop him either.

Our post-coital moments were times of greatest intimacy, and I thought I could alert him to the state of his mother's health during one of those quiet

213

periods. But his inevitable cry, "Oh my gosh, oh my gosh!" disarmed me every time. And I let those tender episodes linger in silence or sweet talk.

Once again a current in his thoughts had slipped by my sixth sense.

"I'm going to draw a map of the area around Janet's spring, your property," he announced after one Saturday afternoon coupling in front of the fireplace, dormant in summer.

"OK. You *are* in the map business, I guess."

"I've seen how they draw up topographical maps at the U.S. Geological Survey, their instruments. It's all done with aerial photographs and 3-D glasses."

I sat up and leaned back against the sofa. "I went to one of those 3-D movies, *House Of Wax*, years ago. Remember that?"

"No. I never went to the movies much when I was growing up. It worried my mother sometimes for me to be out."

"Well, it had Vincent Price, a horror show. But I also saw *It Came From Outer Space*. This was when I was visiting family down near Poplar Spring. In that one, an alien spacecraft flew right at you and crashed. We all ducked and covered our faces!"

I chuckled at the memory. My cousins were younger than I, so I had had to be the calm one. I kept reminding them it was all a movie. It wasn't real, and I knew everything would turn out okay.

"I don't know how they do those things for the movies, and I don't like sci-fi stuff anyway. The Survey mapper looks through an instrument at the aerial photos. He guides a beam of light around the hills and valleys. And the machine, through some sort of linkage, draws the contour lines on a piece of paper." Here he unfolded a map onto the coffee table beside us. "Contour lines connect points of the same elevation."

"Right. The mostly parallel lines." I pointed. "These that are more of a circle are a hill."

"Well, most of them. Where you're pointing is a sinkhole, but the shape of the lines is similar. They're just going down in elevation, not up. Anyway, the mapper starts with a known elevation . . . I've told you about bench marks, right?"

"Right."

"Well, he starts there and he'll do the whole area. It's only where the land is real flat, the desert or prairie, that the instruments don't work. There you have to have a field crew on the ground."

I wondered for a moment why they stopped making those 3-D movies. I guess the novelty wore off, and we went back to the more familiar two-dimensional cinema. Maybe people don't want to feel that things are flying at them all the time.

"OK, but do you think Janet wants a topo map of the spring? Or is it for me?"

"Well, it would be for anyone, but you two should be the most interested. I mean, if you don't decide to live on it, and, you know, sell, you'd still have something. It's going to be a really detailed, well drawn map.

"Yeah," I chuckled. "I can look at it and say, 'I could have had all this! A place where Mickey Mouse and Donald Duck would be happy." I paused. "Do you think it would really work for Janet, though? It can't be the same as the real thing, her childhood."

"A map will last forever."

"But, Louis, when you lose something important, a picture just isn't enough. It's dead, you know? I mean it can't do anything, it just . . . it just lies there."

"No, a map's permanent. It doesn't go anywhere. You always have it."

Here was my chance to tell him he was going to lose the person dearest to him and that no map or drawing or picture would ever replace her. But I couldn't get the words out of my mouth. And when the phone rang the next morning, I knew at the sound of the bell that his mother was gone.

Freddy's Story VIII: *Bodies of Water*

Janet's confrontation with her parents was worse than the revelation by Mrs. Anderson.

"It's not just that they want to make money as investors," she complained to me. Again, we were at The DC, though I had plans to be somewhere else with her later the same day. It was Friday, and we would both be getting off work at 4:00.

"What do you mean?"

"They actually think Hillbillyville will be good for Fairfield, for Phipps County. They were mad when I objected to the whole idea."

"They're in favor of development, then, growth, jobs, expansion."

Developing our relationship, by the way, was my goal right now. I had proposed that Janet ride down to High Hill with me this evening. As it would be a long summer evening, we could get to my favorite ledge well before dark.

"But there are other things they could put their money into," Janet went on. "Hospital services, for instance. There are so many things we can't do here, and people have to go to St. Louis for them--tests and surgeries. We have one of the few glaucoma centers anywhere, out on Kingshighway. And it always needs more money for expansion. We need teams of specialists."

One of her points was sound: the hospital did begin to grow in later years, serving many of the counties bordering Fairfield's. Better roads and more efficient ambulance service brought accident victims for emergency care and patients to outpatient and long term treatment. The development of new drugs and laser surgery at larger institutions, however, left our local eye hospital behind, and it finally had to close.

"Your dad isn't thinking simply of more business for himself, is he, for a doctor?"

"That certainly could be part of it: money. My mom wants to improve the country club. More and fancier functions. She also wants to hold elegant social events in our house, and that means new furniture, serving pieces, paintings, you name it."

"That's not a worry at my house! Dad wants business, but he doesn't seem driven to build up the home place."

On the phone earlier that week, I had found myself inviting Janet for a drive down to the family farm, but I hadn't asked her to meet any of my family. Why, I wasn't sure. After I'd done it, I realized Janet, who loved to hike and to be outdoors, would like climbing High Hill. But what was I trying to show her from the top? It couldn't be a view that gave her pleasure.

"There's also their idea to buy a Lake of the Ozarks place," Janet said suddenly, pointing a finger at me as if I'd been trying to hide this fact from her. "I should have known that!"

Lake of the Ozarks is one of the world's largest manmade lakes, more than one hundred miles long with a shore over a thousand miles. Many professional people like the Masters aspired to vacation homes on that water.

All along Route 66 you could see billboards picturing bikini clad water skiers skimming the lake's surface and attractive young couples admiring spectacular sunsets from the decks of houses that resembled Swiss chalets. Most people at this time saw it all as part of the healthy development of Missouri's tourist industry. Looking back, I see many forces behind the Lake's creation--electric power, of course, was one of the most important.

Bagnell Dam was built in the early 1930s, spilling the Osage River into the valleys of central Missouri. This region, like the rest of the country, was in the first grip of the Depression. And people from my area knew the building of the dam meant much needed jobs. Eventually there would be recreational facilities, too, motels, summer cottages, and camps all producing money and jobs. But we didn't foresee other effects of the whole project.

Whenever I look out over that water even now, I tend to imagine submerged barns, fenced in underwater pastures, a depopulated Ozark Atlantis. But even I didn't understand for a long time the way in which the growing enterprise would transform the lives of those whose land was preserved.

After all, a primary goal of the dam in the first place was electricity for St. Louis, the major urban center to the east. But more electricity there meant more capacity for homes and industry, more businesses and employees. And city residents often want places to go for weekend getaways. That led to highways and traffic slicing into quiet rural territory and changing a once remote, simple people. Lake of the Ozarks--and other artificially created lakes, Bull Shoals, Pomme de Terre, Table Rock, Taneycomo-- brought the city to the country in the Show Me State.

Janet's parents were like many city dwellers who wanted vacation residences featuring glassed-in porches, lawns manicured by a gardening service, paved driveways, and all the amenities of houses in fine suburban neighborhoods. So what spread out from the shores of Lake of the Ozarks looked more and more like an upscale development in wealthy St. Louis County, a sharp contrast to the simple farms and villages that had been in place there for generations.

Now Janet and I--and Bobby and Louis--saw the American drive to civilize the wilderness slithering overland from Lake of the Ozarks toward Fairfield and a future Hillbillyville. To us, it was a snake swollen with poison, a weedy root tunneling underground to suck water and nutrients from weaker vegetation. We gasped at our own bold attempt to stop it.

Janet gasped at the view from High Hill.

"Oh, it's like a preview of Hillbillyville!"

"Yeah. Over that way, it's sad. But when I was a kid, the view was pretty good. You have to focus from this line over to the west. It's such beautiful country, but you have to ignore the torn up spots."

"Hmm."

"You can imagine what it was like when I first came here, after leaving the Circle. That's more than fifteen years ago."

We were sitting in the late afternoon sun, the rocks warm beneath us and the little stream from the mountain spring murmuring its way downhill.

"I suppose it could look that way again," Janet mused. "If you filled in those holes, moved the rusted equipment away, planted new trees."

"Well, it would take quite a bit. Can you rebuild mountains or would they just be piles of rocks? And how long does it take for a forest to recover, fifty years, a hundred?"

"A long time, sure. Is that a pond you had put in?"

"Oh, no. We were just digging the limestone, and that made a low place the water filled in."

"Ugh! Looks like a cess pool. It's so stagnant, there's stuff growing in it."

"I spent a day out there fishing once before my dad told me there was nothing to catch."

"Wouldn't it be nice, though, if the old place could be restored? Maybe you could give the land to the county, and it would become a park. Some place for families to come and have picnics, for grade school classes to go on trips in the spring, or old folks to drive out early in the morning to birdwatch."

"No, problem. I'll tell my parents to move back to Fairfield and stay with the Potters!"

"Oh, don't be silly. I'm just daydreaming. But look here: where the lane comes in to your house, if you just...."

And as she talked something beautiful took shape in our minds, a park that wasn't completely wild but wasn't all fences and walls either. There was one road in but a number of hiking paths branching out to wander through the property. A few rustic structures gave visitors places to get information, set up picnics, rest in the shade. Here was a wildlife observation area, there a small field of wildflowers.

I saw this scene in my mind as a combination of my own memories and visions of a grand future. But I also saw in the present the girl who was painting the picture with such passion.

"Janet," I said when she paused. "I want to go into business in Fairfield and I want to help you stop Hillbillyville and I want you and me to be together."

Bobby's Story VIII:
Synchronization

Of course, I broke off my study for the law boards and my research into legal provisions of inheritance in order to be with Louis. He had no family besides his mother, and he fell apart.

It didn't happen immediately, however. He was oddly calm taking the phone call that Sunday afternoon, and he assured me he would be okay driving back to Fairfield. I didn't believe him and insisted on traveling behind him in my truck. I also called Janet before we left. I felt the dam would burst soon enough.

Janet already knew about Mrs. Clark's death and was quick to say she would do whatever she could to help Louis. She also relayed some important new information about Hillbillyville, so it was good for me to have time alone behind the wheel. I could get my mental dowsing rod out to find which way things were moving.

I figured that Martin Flint had approached investors, including important citizens of Fairfield, as if he already owned the property west of town. He didn't know anything about me, the official heir, except that I lived in Lost Spring, Missouri. So he assumed I could be duped. Money would dazzle the barefoot mountain girl who, at fifteen, had probably married an overall-wearing, tobacco-chewing moonshiner, perhaps a first cousin.

My responses to Flint had been brief, politely rejecting each offer without revealing either my own legal knowledge or my awareness of the scheme's endorsement by Midwestern and Eastern backers. I knew I'd have to emerge from behind a disguise of rural ignorance at some point. But I wanted the four of us young people to have time to come up with a plan that would satisfy my Great Aunt's terms of inheritance. Freddy Sill was the one who discovered Flint's presence in Fairfield and gave me warning of that group's next move.

Martin Flint was a guy Freddy called "Mr. Briefcase" who'd been staying at Stony Court Motel. On the last day of Sill Rock Company's work there, removing Ozark Giraffe, Freddy overhead an exchange between Flint and a woman named Helen Street: they had contacted my parents and were arranging a deal. Or so it appeared to Freddy and Janet, who told me all about it. I couldn't believe my parents would be party to such an underhanded maneuver.

"I've got the deal," Martin had said to Miss Street. Freddy was sitting on a small sofa in the motel lobby, waiting for his dad to come out of a meeting with Mr. Bachmann. They were settling accounts now that the job was complete.

"The Greens have agreed?" asked Street.

"Yes. They say they can make the daughter go along. But damn them, they've screwed up the price! Still, we'll make it back in the long run."

"I can get the papers together by the morning. Where do we mail them?"

"No mail. They want us to come to Lost Spring, wherever the hell in the boondocks that is!"

Up to this point, Freddy was just listening because he had nothing else to do until his dad emerged from Bachmann's office. But then he heard the telltale word come out of Flint's mouth.

"We ought to keep these people as residents of Hillbillyville. We wouldn't have to buy them costumes or teach them any dialect. Hicks, if I ever heard any."

"Well, we'd better be cordial while we're down there. Our people are getting suspicious that we're not inviting investors in to see the land or scheduling a groundbreaking. The Green daughter has held us up, though we've made some use of that time."

She chuckled oddly at her own remark. Briefcase went on, "I couldn't get her parents on the phone until this week. Actually, they called me, probably from the 'Lost Spring's General Store.'"

I don't think Freddy knew at this time that my folks had been traveling overseas. So some parts of this overheard conversation didn't make sense to him. But he took in everything that was said after the word, "Hillbillyville."

His conclusion was that my folks were going to make me sell out, somehow having learned that the price for Aunt Betsy's land was going up and up and up. I had mentioned the latest offer when they checked in by phone. But I did say to them that I wasn't crazy about the plans this group had for development. Given their love for their own country home, I never thought they'd join forces with the people behind Hillbillyville.

Since my parents were due back in less than 48 hours--but it was possible I'd have to stay in Fairfield--I figured I needed Janet and Freddy's help to block any Hillbillyville transaction. If they had concluded I'd be more prepared for the future with cash rather than with property, I wouldn't be angry with them. But the full story ought to get to them as soon as possible.

Fortunately, Janet was due a holiday, and Sill Rock Company was shutting down for a few days after the rush to finish at Stony Court. They agreed to drive down to Lost Spring and meet my parents, carrying a brief note from me. The detailed explanation would come in conversation. That trip, born of necessity, later proved an important event in the emergence of our final plan, the creation of Route 66 Spring.

Louis had kept his emotions bottled up during the three hours he was on the road back to Fairfield. When we arrived at his address in Fairfield Gardens and he found the house empty (his mother's remains were already at the funeral home), sobs rose up from so deep in him he could no longer stand.

Mrs. Clark had had a weak heart, a condition discovered several years earlier by Dr. Masters. In those days there was no treatment, and they both knew it could happen in an instant. She fell in the grocery store, her hand still clutching the box of laundry detergent she'd been ready to add to her cart.

Louis learned all this on the phone at my house, but, of course, it didn't sink in until he opened the front door. He was not even able to go the funeral home until the next morning. I spent that night with him and promised to stay the week.

That may have been the time I acknowledged that my feelings for Louis had merged into a stronger current. And I know the timepieces of the Clark household eased me into that realization over the course of my week's stay.

Mr. Clark had been a jeweler, but a jeweler with a special fascination for watches, clocks, hourglasses, anything that recorded the passage of time. Louis told me that his shop, Don Quixote's, used to be dizzying with its array of different grandfather, desktop, and wall clocks. They gonged, binged, and chimed at quarter-hour, half-hour, and hourly intervals, but not simultaneously. Each ran on its own inner schedule, faster or slower than its neighbors.

According to her son, Mrs. Clark had saved only a representative sample from her husband's collection, But each of the little rooms in that small house had timepieces on furniture, walls, and shelves ticking and tocking to their own inner rhythms.

I slept that week on the living room sofa, as Louis' room had only one single bed and neither of us wanted to use his mother's room. It was, though, a tiny house, so I wasn't far from Louis and awoke frequently to hear him thrashing in his bed. Though he didn't call me, I went to him each time.

I also woke sometimes to the living room's most conspicuous timepiece, a coocoo clock that rested on the top of a corner cabinet next to the dining room. The mechanism that opened the little door through which a tiny bird emerged to sing the hours' passing groaned and strained for at least thirty seconds at the top of every hour. Its mournful cry, "Coocoo, Coocoo, Coocoo," pulled me from the dozing state I lay in most of the night.

I tell you, that many clocks will make anyone think about how she's spending her time! Before Louis came to Uncle Carter's, I'd been coasting through this summer, vaguely anticipating the end of study, my law license, a job somewhere. But I wasn't moving purposely towards any of those things.

Louis believed he was marching along a path he'd set out on some years earlier, his training as an engineer, field jobs, an office position, the comfortable, secure world of corporate management. Meeting me had thrown him off schedule, though he wouldn't admit it. And during midnight wakefulness in the Clark house I realized that the only stable figure within the structure of advancing time was the union of the two of us.

Freddy's Story IX: Lucy's Spring

I could tell Janet was startled by my unplanned confession that I was attracted to her. With her campaign to stop Hillbillyville the prime focus of her life at that moment, she wasn't ready to make any commitment beyond friendship.

"For right now, let's just be childhood pals who've gotten together again after a decade and a half."

"Sure, I understand, sure. Associates, maybe. You're helping me look into going into business around here, and I'm helping you find out if there's a way to preserve your spring. Buddies, business associates."

I realized I'd been carried away up on High Hill. That place held so many good memories of childhood for me that I had let my guard down. The truth slipped out.

"I'm putting things together here, you know," said Janet. "My parents being investors. I hadn't known that, the past. I like to know how things got to be the way they are."

"Sure. I want to find out how everyone stands too."

"I'm not seeing anyone else, you know. I had been dating, earlier in the summer . . . Brad . . . "

"Oh, I had a girlfriend in the spring. She's back home. Anyway, I've got to concentrate on finding work in Fairfield. Mr. Taylor and Mr. Stephens, out at Cool's Pool, have given me a couple of people to get in touch with. There are possibilities."

"There's something else that's bothering me about this Hillbillyville thing too. It's Mrs. Anderson."

"What do you mean?"

"Well, she's usually such a wild card, someone who doesn't go along with what everyone else says. And there's her love of animals. I would have predicted that she'd be picketing the site rather than telling me to accept the inevitable."

"Maybe you should talk to her again."

"I'm going to. I'm going to. But right now I guess we'd better come down from the mountain." She offered me a sweet smile and one of her rich laughs. And they gave me hope.

I dropped Janet off at her house before the summer sun had set completely and then, as dark settled in, turned my truck back down Route 66 toward home. While she had reaffirmed her plan of talking to Sophie Anderson, I realized I should speak to my folks about the future. Mostly, I meant my splitting off into my own line of work. But I had also begun to wonder if Sill Rock Company had made any deals with the Hillbillyville people.

I'd looked carefully at the landscape west of Fairfield and saw a very rocky terrain. Building a theme park there would mean blasting and removing rock before bulldozers could start putting dirt where it was wanted. There would be big money for someone.

My father was a quiet man, given to few but strong words. So I didn't think he'd disguise his intentions.

"Freddy," he said when I spoke to him about what was next for the company. "I'm thinking of turning to farming."

"Farming!" We'd always had a vegetable garden, sometimes a single cow, generally a small flock of chickens. But it was my mother who managed all that.

"I've been looking around the place," he swept an arm toward the front porch. "There's a lot that's too much hill, but we've got fields enough. And we don't have to make it big, just keep a little money coming in. I might want to raise sheep."

"You've always been so . . . so determined in work. I thought you enjoyed it."

"That was true when we started, after the war. And it paid the bills, sent your older brothers to school." My brothers were eight and ten years older, more like uncles to me. They'd gone to college and now lived and worked in Springfield. "But lately, I don't know, it's kind of getting me down."

"Long days, tired body?"

"It's more the holes in the ground I keep leaving. They've started to bother me. In the beginning they were so much better than the holes I was making back in the war." He paused, and his gaze went past me to the darkened window. He'd never talked much about his Army days. He had no photos of his unit, and he never attended a reunion with buddies. I wasn't sure exactly what he had done as a soldier.

"I thought you . . . um . . . built up as well as tore up. Roads and all."

Another pause. "That wasn't my specialty."

And that was pretty much all he would say and, in one sense, all I needed to know as far as the current situation was involved. Much later I learned more about my father's past and came to understand why he did, in fact, retire by the end of this same year. What I found out made me proud.

Janet, on the other hand, was more saddened by what she learned about her old friend Sophie Anderson. Beneath the surface of this surprisingly energetic elderly lady, Janet found a tired and frustrated woman. I heard her history later that week.

"We were in her kitchen," Janet explained, "with the gerbils, who were burrowing in the wood shavings, and the hamsters running in their wheels."

"Did you mention the animals that would have no home in Hillbillyville, no places to run?"

"I started to, but she got to talking about the past, her past. There are things I didn't know. She really was lost when her husband died and her children were gone from home. She wanted to start a business, a way of occupying her time."

"Well, I guess she did it, with those laboratory animals."

"Yeah, but that came later. At first she tried to run a dress shop, and then she thought she could sell insurance. She says men in this town didn't want women running businesses."

"Things are changing now, though."

"Well, some. That's what she told me, that I would have it easier in my lifetime. Somewhere in there she told me more about Lucy Rivers Johns, my lady of the spring."

"Oh?"

"Mrs. Anderson admired her independence, her fire. Of course, Lucy had money. And that was in the 1920s, a time when women, the flappers, were rebelling."

"I bet there weren't any flappers in Fairfield!"

"Probably not. But Lucy had learned how to be forceful in New York. Sophie felt this woman could have owned her own store and found customers. But Lucy mostly just came into town, toured the countryside talking about the good old days, and left."

"Did Mrs. Anderson learn from her friend how to be tougher?"

"I suppose so, but Sophie's resources were drastically reduced during the Depression. Her house was paid for, and that kept her here while her sons struggled elsewhere."

"How did she get into the lab animals business?"

"That's a funny part: she wrote a prospectus under the name of 'S. Anderson.' The suppliers believed she was a man."

"Clever. When was this?"

"Must have been during the war. And that explains part of it, as men were off fighting and lots of women replaced them in factories and elsewhere."

"So, she got her own business at last."

"Well, not entirely. During the early years she had to borrow to get stock. She began to make money, but, with supplies needed, unexpected losses, she never made enough to pay back her creditors. So the business has always been only part hers."

"Who owns the rest?"

"You might guess: for years, Lucy Rivers Johns. She made the initial loan. She was trying to get Sophie to act as an agent for her in some secret land deal. She wanted property in this area that people didn't want her to have. I think Sophie finally bought it for her, but she wouldn't come out and say it directly."

"Wait a minute, you don't suppose the land she bought is the land that's come down to Bobby?"

"I don't know. She didn't say."

"You do realize what it would mean if she did, don't you?"

"It would mean my spring is Lucy's spring! And that bottle, with her letter in it, which she dropped in a creek or river somewhere between here and St. Louis, came back home. So now I've got to save this spring for both of us!"

Bobby's Story IX: Allies

I didn't know the outcome of Street's and Flint's trip to Lost Spring until several days after their meeting with my parents. Louis needed me at the funeral and the meetings with his mother's lawyer and insurance agent. While I worried about what was going on back home, I decided to wait for word to come to me.

Along with neighbors from Fairfield Gardens and a handful of church members, Freddy and Janet were also at Mrs. Clark's funeral. They met with Louis and me several times later in the week as we put together the scheme that in the end saved Lucy Rivers Johns's spring.

Seeing after Louis's affairs ironically led us to information about Miss Street that significantly helped our cause. It seemed she had some quirky tastes in lovemaking. And if we had revealed what we knew, local investors were likely to back away. In the end, we didn't have to spread gossip: it went by itself.

While Louis was hearing details about his inheritance (the house was his and some modest savings toward the remainder of his college education), I chatted with Mr. Jenkins' secretary.

"I hear you're not happy with that theme park they want to build," Mrs. Feibelman said. "He," she jerked her head back to indicate her boss. "He was going in, but now he's pulled out."

"Why's that?"

"It probably has something to do with what I told him."

When she didn't continue, I realized it was my job to insist on hearing Mrs. Feibelman's story. "So you knew something about the plan? Was it unsound, some problem with surface drainage or underground water flow?"

"No," she said, leaning forward and lowering her voice. "It was one of the women from out of town, Miss Street, her name is."

"Oh?" I knew from Freddy that she was involved, but I had assumed she was just an administrative assistant, someone who got the papers all straight.

"You know, Belle, down at Hair Today, Gone Tomorrow?"

"No." I didn't know her or the Hair thing, which turned out to be a local beauty shop. The more I talked here, the more I felt I was moving away from what I wanted to know.

"Well, Belle, she does Mrs. Arnold's hair. Mrs. Arnold keeps horses, out in the county. And one day they were both in there, Mrs. Arnold and Miss Street. Miss Street found out about her having horses and all, so they left together."

"To ride horses?" The answer to my real question seemed to have ridden off on the runaway horse of this account!

"That's what I thought, of course. But it wasn't that. Miss Street wanted equipment."

"From what I've heard, she didn't seem the outdoor type. Wasn't she always dressed up, all business?"

"During the day, sure. But at night, according to Sandy, who does rooms over at the Stony Court, at night she likes to play games. Pretend, like."

"Mrs. Feibelman, I'm sorry but I don't see what you're getting at. What did Sandy tell Belle--or was it Mrs. Arnold who told Belle, who told you?"

"I've been getting to it all along, sweetie. This Street woman liked to dress up like a cowboy. Boots and hat and pants."

"Well, that is a bit strange." Of course, as kids we'd all had cowboy and Indian outfits, David Crocket, Tonto, Annie Oakley. There was probably a skirt with fringes up in my parents' attic.

Mrs. Feibleman leaned even closer now and spoke yet more softly. "The last thing she put on was . . . spurs. That's what she wanted from Mrs. Arnold."

This made some sense, though why it was important in the midst of her group's effort to secure Hillbillyville seemed odd.

"And then . . . " Mrs. Feibelman said this softest of all. "And then she rode that business partner of hers, Mr. Flint."

The picture this created in a flash of imagination was enough to make my head snap back. I know my eyes were wide, and my mouth probably fell open. I got those parts of my face under control just seconds before Louis stepped out of Mr. Jenkins' office.

237

What he had found out was hardly as surprising as what I'd learned, but it did assure him that he could afford to take some time--a month or more, easily--to decide what he would do now. He claimed the big question was whether or not he would go back to school in the fall. But I knew that, beneath the surface of his talk, he was questioning his whole scheme for the future.

I thought it might be good to get Louis out of town for a few days to think all this out. He agreed to go with me to Lost Spring, where we could hear firsthand what had transpired with the architects of Hillbillyville.

Louis met my parents first, appropriately, at River's Bend.

"You've lived in Arkansas County all your lives?" he asked as we were all getting acquainted. They had expressed sympathy at his mom's death and realized he was a bit at loose ends. This question from Louis was a good sign, though. His mind's eye was viewing a topographic map of the region as he tried to pinpoint the location of wells on our property.

"That's right. But in recent years, we've traveled, seen the world." Our salads arrived at the table.

"Italy, right?" I noticed that Louis ordered the catfish.

"We spent the last six weeks in a villa outside of Florence. Mother wanted to see the art. But you know what? We found we were more interested in the grapes they grow around there, the vineyards and the orchards."

"We used to farm," I added. "Until some investments paid off really well. We lease the land now."

"It's nice down here," Louis offered. "Earlier in the summer, I was just working this area. But now I see how pretty things are, the long ridges, the deep valleys. Parts are a bit wild, of course."

Both of my parents chuckled at this. "Not if you've grown up here," my dad said.

"That brings up a question," I began. "You know I've always loved it in Lost Spring, and I came to really dislike the city, all its traffic and hustle. So I hate to see outsiders come into our region and try to modernize."

"You're talking about Hillbillyville, I bet."

"Well, yeah. Do you know all about it, what they want to do with that land Aunt Betsy left for me?"

"Of course, we do, dear," Mom said.

"So, you understand that I wouldn't want to see it go to investors from Chicago and Boston? They would make a mockery of the Ozarks."

"That's why we had those people, Mr. Flint and Miss Street, down here," explained my dad. "To make them understand who they were dealing with."

"You don't mean you were making a deal for me, do you?"

"Of course not! After we learned from your friends, Janet and Freddy, what Flint was talking about, we explained that you had your own plans for the property. We said that we and some of our friends were going to invest in them along with you."

"But I don't have plans!"

"You're going to preserve the spring, of course."

"The spring? Well, yes, there is a spring on the property, but what do you know about it."

"That's the land your Great Aunt Betsy's mother grew up on, where her grandfather built an iron works when people from the East were moving out here. And she had a beautiful house, an elegant garden, a spring that her father pumped water from up to his fancy house. She told us about it years ago."

"Oh, so it *is* a family place. I guess I do have to keep it. But, you know, I don't really want to live there, and that's a problem with the will, a stipulation. What I've come to realize this summer is I belong in Lost Spring."

"Well, dear," concluded my mother. "You're a lawyer. You'll figure something out." And, indeed, that's just what I did.

Later, as the four of us leaned back in our chairs, stuffed with good country cooking, including rich blackberry pie, I realized something else about my future. I'd had more reasons for bringing Louis here than keeping his mind off of loss, though that was important. I had wanted him, I realized, to meet my parents.

Freddy's Story X: The Pipe

My father's decision to wind down his rock business and begin farming created the perfect opportunity for me to see how far my expertise in Ozark Giraffe would carry me. It would mean, I assumed at first, piecing together a lot of little jobs to establish my reputation around Phipps County. I didn't anticipate, however, that a single big project would make me well known as a rock carver in just a few years.

Janet uncovered this project and told me about it while we were making yet another visit to her spring. This time, rather than approaching off Route 66, we hiked from her house in the Circle. I believe it was probably during the time when Bobby and Louis were talking to her parents down in Lost Spring.

"I guess I have to tell you what else I found about about Mrs. Anderson," Janet said resignedly. We were heading into the woods past the edge of the neighborhood.

"About her being unable to fulfill Lucy's plan to preserve her family's land?"

"Well, yes and no. She did buy that property--this property we're walking to almost surely--for her friend. But she also received payment of sorts."

"Lucy canceled her business loan?"

"No, she gave Mrs. Anderson a small parcel of land. Can you guess where that piece is?" We had paused at the point where the little-used gravel road ended. We had to move now single file down a path through brush and small trees.

I thought for a minute, then realized there could only be one answer to Janet's question. "She's got the section that provides access, the little stretch right along Route 66!"

"That's right. Flint gave her a handsome sum for it."

"You mean it's already sold? When did this happen?"

"I guess it was back in the spring, when Bobby's Aunt Betsy was failing. He had checked into the will and knew he would need to secure access to his proposed building site, assuming he could buy Bobby out of her inheritance."

"And back then Mrs. Anderson wouldn't have had any idea of the larger scheme."

"Well, I'm not so sure of that. She's cagey, as I've told you. And the money she got has more than freed her from debt. What she didn't foresee was my objection to the whole scheme."

"And Bobby's love of Missouri's natural beauty." I waved an arm at the view in front of us. We had come out into the clearing around the abandoned house, and, from the ridge top, it offered a fine view to the west. "I wonder if we can confirm this as the house Luther Johns built, where Lucy spent her childhood."

"Well, we've determined this is the land, but I don't know if this is the actual site for the house."

"I think I know a way to find out," I said. "I need to get around to the other side, above the spring." The path to the spring we had followed before wound out to the west side of the ridge, avoiding the vertical cliff above the bubbling pool. This was, we believe, the cliff from which one of the James' gang, in pursuit of Oroginee, had jumped to his death.

"You see what you can find there. I'm going down to the spring itself."

It took me less than ten minutes to locate what I was looking for, though I didn't announce it to Janet for nearly an hour. What she called up from the spring below made me forget for a time what I had discovered.

"Here's what I think,"' she began. I could hear Janet perfectly, the words rising up from where she stood, unseen at the water's edge. "First, we convince Bobby to keep the land and promise to preserve it by dedicating this property to the public's use in its present form."

"You mean, make it into a park? I'm not sure Phipps County or the town of Fairfield is going to want a park out here, away from everything."

"Ah, but that's the key!" Her excitement rose as she continued. "First, it's not 'away from everything.' And second, it's not just for this area. This park will be for everyone in America. It's going to be a memorial to the nation's history of starting fresh, rejecting worn out institutions--England's monarchy, for instance--and beginning again, with democracy."

"Ah, and America's frontier. 'Go west, young man, go west.'"

"Recover the Garden of Eden!"

"Well, that might work, the Garden of Eden, because we're out here in the middle of nowhere."

"But we're not in the middle of nowhere! It's right on Route 66, the symbol of America, our 'Main Street,' 'the Mother Road.' We're going to call what I'm standing beside 'Route 66 Spring!'"

I peered down into the leaves and branches of the bushes that hung on the side of the cliff above the spring. "Ah, and get travelers to stop here on their way across the country."

"Right. You see, we make a drive in from Route 66 to the farmhouse ruin, where we build a visitor's center. Then we construct a circular walkway." I could feel her pointing, even though I couldn't see her. "And then up the other side."

"I see how you could put in a visitor's center, a little nature walk. But will people come?"

"They will if we make it a story, actually two stories."

"Luther Taylor Johns and one of the first iron works west of the Mississippi?"

"Yes, how people brought the means of a better life to this part of the New World. But also the story of how Sacagawea saved an Osage princess from a rampaging James gang member."

"You might be stretching the truth there a bit, you know."

"Hmm. Well, we'll see. I'll do more research. In any case, the spring will be a symbol of hope, of humanity's eternal need to believe that the world can be made a better place."

"You might be on to something. There may be as many people wanting to celebrate genuine heroes rather than stock characters, Daisy Mae and Lil' Abner of Hillbillyville."

"That's what I'm counting on, numbers. All those people driving down Route 66, seeing America. They'll be like the ants that come after Leiniger, but it will be Flint and Street they gobble up. What we need to do too is advertise."

Again, her voice rose with enthusiasm. "Just like the Burma Shave signs, all along the highway getting people's attention." She hesitated and I knew she was trying to compose a set of signs on the spot. (She couldn't come up with one that day but later proudly announced the first of many jingles that would appear on Missouri's roadsides in later years: 'Don't drive so fast / you go right past / the next best thing / Route 66 Spring!')

"I'm willing to help," I called down, "but don't ask me to write stuff!"

"Oh, you know what you can do, anyway, don't you?"

"Well, I can . . . " I paused not just because I didn't understand my projected role in this enterprise, but also because I'd found what I was looking for. At least I thought I had.

"You can do everything in Ozark Giraffe, like the wall of the Cool's Pool. I love that look, and it's so typical of the area. We'll need not just a visitor's center, but the walk to the spring. Why, even the little drive in from Route 66 should have neat rock walls lining the way. And around the parking area."

"Whoa! I'd love to work on these things, but now you're talking money. A lot of money just to build, and then how do you keep the whole thing going? Are you charging admission?"

"Yes, there's a lot to figure out. But what I see is setting up a foundation, a private fund. If Bobby owns the land--and then wills it to the foundation-- we'll be able to make Route 66 Spring last forever."

"Don't forget the will says she has to live on the land. And even you are not sure she wants to do that."

"OK, I admit there are some points to work on. Oh, and Flint has to give up Mrs. Anderson's strip of land. He's not going to sell to me once he realizes I've sabotaged Hillbillyville."

I didn't respond to this concession that her dream was looking a bit like a pipe dream because . . . well, because I'd found Luther Rivers Johns' dream pipe. "Hey, Janet, come up here. I've got something to show you."

Bobby's Story X: National Treasure

For more than forty years I have lived on Turtleback every day of the month but one. Twelve nights a year I stay in what we call the "guest house" at Route 66 Spring, although I own it and all the property. While this arrangement probably isn't exactly what Great Aunt Betsy had anticipated in her will, it fulfills the spirit of her bequest: we've saved her mother's land.

The legal loophole we slipped through involved "maintaining a residence," but it has helped that no one ever challenged our interpretation of that phrase. With the help of some other lawyers, I carved a legal document that established the Johns Foundation and that will turn this land over to the organization at my death. The trust fund built over three decades should cover maintenance for as far as we can see into the future.

Martin Flint was willing to sell the piece of property he'd purchased from Sophie Anderson at a small loss. He was eager to disappear from Fairfield after the story of his being saddled and ridden by Helen Street popped up in barbershop and beauty parlor. And she . . . well, Helen was bought off by Gene Chapman.

My father's old Army buddy was the *deus ex machina* that took care of loose ends we young plotters had failed to anticipate. He brought first an electronic industry and then a software development outfit to Phipps County, creating enough business to offset any lost earnings from a Hillbillyville. And when Miss Street, less afraid of publicity than was her partner, threatened to be trouble about the deal gone sour, Gene helped her land a lucrative position in a Chicago corporation. I'm pretty sure she was never happy there, though, or at any in the series of jobs she moved through over the next decades.

Not only did Chapman Technologies create jobs for the area, it also inspired the college's electrical engineering program to establish co-op training programs, bringing out-of-state students and new residents to the area. Too, travelers down Route 66 represented a significant tourist industry, which didn't degrade our way of life or belittle our heritage.

Of course, we were setting up the spring just as old Route 66 was dying to provide the path for Interstate 44. But the Mother Road has had a remarkable ability to rise from its own ashes in the form of Historic Route 66, a regional obsession gone national, and now international. Submerged for a time, the ideas behind America's Main Street worked their way to the surface of our nation's consciousness just as surely and steadily as our state's rainwater moves from sinkhole to cave to river to spring.

Janet and Freddy still run Route 66 Spring: she the visionary who saw the shape of past, present, and future; he the architect, builder, repairman who keeps the operation grounded. This happily married couple regularly welcome seven grandchildren among the stream of visitors coming to or passing through Fairfield. Even in heavy winter, few days pass when at least one car containing a family member doesn't wind in from the highway.

The park closes at dusk, however, so at night Route 66 Spring turns back into Lucy Rivers Johns' favorite location for communion with nature. I've just come back myself from a moonlit, midnight walk around the spring, a slow one now at my age. If I'm pokey, though, I'm not alone, as Louis is at my side.

From the beginning my husband has kept the records for this modest operation. At first Freddy and Janet were mailing packets down to Turtleback on Friday, and we called back budget information by telephone early in the following week. But two decades ago we computerized the operation, and Louis now does the books and maintains the Spring's online website from Turtleback.

Louis, Freddy, and I have been the workers in this project, but it is Janet who first dreamed it all. She recognized the importance of symbols to a people, the representations of hope, progress, and achievement. She knew that great symbols are simple things like springs, water forever emerging from the earth to nourish a landscape and its inhabitants. Such national treasures not only commemorate past events but also inspire great futures.

Sure, Freddy had to build and then maintain the visitors' center, the rock walkway down to the spring, the Ozark Giraffe walls lining the drive and picnic areas. I crafted the documents that maintain the park's nonprofit status and its goal of public service. Louis records everything from our monthly number of visitors to the spring's daily output, from the Foundation's trust fund investment return to the nature of odd items occasionally bubbling to the spring's surface.

But Janet created the slide show about Oroginee and Sacagawea, the working tabletop model of Luther Johns' pioneering iron works, the onsite re-creation of Lucy John's mother's frontier garden. And she melded these histories from the last century

with the twentieth-century legend of America's most famous highway, Route 66. So even travelers who stop just to use the restroom usually leave with an unanticipated sense of purpose derived from ancestors who faced and overcame great challenges.

Earlier this evening Janet told Louis and me we were too old to be taking a midnight stroll down to the spring. But I countered that they could get inspiration from the spring every day of the year, while I had to make the most of my monthly opportunities. We'd proposed the hike after dinner at the curator's house, where they live.

"Besides," Janet said in a final response. "I'm worried another bottle will pop to the surface and present me with a new mission!" She gave us one of those long deep laughs that signal satisfaction and pleasure deeply felt.

It has given me great pleasure to be one of the founders of Route 66 Spring, though I've lived the great bulk of my life at a distance from the real operation. A part-time research associate of a St. Louis environmental law firm when my children were young and a full time partner once the internet connected remote Arkansas County with the world's data bases, I consider myself remarkably fortunate to live in an ideal place while working to promote greater appreciation of threatened wild places in America.

I had to work to pay back my parents' original purchase of Turtleback. Rather than sell the land outside of Fairfield that I had inherited to get that down payment, I accepted the generous payback schedule they offered. Insisting that I apply myself over a long time to work I could believe in, my dad was following the lesson he'd learned in an early retirement.

I like to think our effort to create and preserve Route 66 Spring as a national landmark resembles Luther Johns' Fantastic Fountain, the gravity-driven hydraulic ram. When Freddy found the pipe and some pieces of the old pump itself, we had yet more confirmation that Janet's spring and Lucy's were one and the same. We also had a material representation of the pioneer spirit.

Using only the power of water traveling downhill, the Fantastic Fountain provides drinking water to a house and irrigation to a garden. We've tried to tap the strength of American ingenuity throughout our history to inspire the belief we can find solutions to new problems. And it works.

As Louis opened the door to the guest house for me a few moments ago (and I powered up my laptop to record these last thoughts before sleep), I believe our journey down the steps, around the spring, and back to the ridge top was not unaccompanied. Since Janet and Freddy had already turned in after dinner, I don't mean they were by our sides.

It's the past that walked with us: Lucy Rivers Johns and Oroginee, John Steinbeck's struggling families fleeing the Dust Bowl, characters played by Martin Milner and George Marahis in their Corvette, fellow citizens and international guests who've gotten their "kicks on Route 66" and gone on to a heavenly reward.

It's a parade the four of us Hillbillyville opponents must join ourselves before too long. But we can hardly regret the hand fate dealt us or the course we forged with our own will and determination after Janet plucked a crusty bottle and a faded letter from the spring's water. We can only hope to leave a similar possibility for the children of the future. As the old century closes on this New Year's Eve and a fresh millennium opens to the world at dawn, each of us remains convinced that this grand story is to be continued.

The End

Epilogue:
Missouri Legends III

Catherine Brooke isn't famous in Missouri history yet, but that's because her memorable accomplishment is so recent we can't fix it in the past. Still, there's little doubt that the woman who walked through a mountain will be a legend in our future.

Catherine epitomized success for a professional woman at the end of the twentieth century: CEO of a significant Kansas City corporation; chair of state and regional charity and foundation boards; recipient of honorary degrees.

She never married, having gently rejected half a dozen offers by the time she slipped away from family and friends at a still youthful 45 years of age. And for much of the previous two decades she had enjoyed the regular company of a respected politician, who later acknowledged his love for this woman.

If she had no family of her own, she was a faithful godmother to the daughters of two old friends, especially after losing her own parents. If you had asked her at almost any point in her career if she was happy, her honest answer would have been "profoundly." So why did she walk away from it all? The answer is growing with her legend, but where it happened is probably the first important clue.

Catherine Brooke disappeared half a mile from Canyon Shut-in in one of the most rugged sections of Missouri. South and west of St. Louis, the area is mountainous, heavily forested, sparsely populated. It's a place for cooking on wood stoves, front porch banjo pickers, the contemplation of lightning bugs and stars.

There are many "shut-ins" in Missouri, places where streams knife through igneous knobs. Constricted to a narrow channel, water rushes through a shut-in, although both before and after it moves within wider beds at a more restrained pace.

It would seem that shut-in water enigmatically choses the hardest path possible, moving from a soft valley directly into rock obstacles rather than wandering around masses of granite. Geologists are sometimes uncertain whether the stream has cut down into such rock from above or found lower fractures through which to make its way. But in all shut-ins leisurely travel is abandoned for a mad race, as water twists and turns, bubbles and splashes, bucks and retreats on its way to a distant destination.

Another feature of shut-ins are potholes, depressions created by gravel caught in tight turns. Small rocks are swirled around and around where water can't move forward directly, carving out larger and larger potholes in the igneous base. Seen from above, then, shut-ins consist of a rocky area with a tortuously twisting path marked by treacherous potholes.

Catherine had taken her older goddaughter, Deborah, a first-year college student, on a daytrip from Fairfield to Canyon Shut-in. They'd packed picnic lunches, worn the appropriate gear for hiking, remembered topographical maps in case they wanted to leave the blazed paths.

"She was whimsical," Deborah told reporters a week later. "She talked about her childhood, growing up in Eureka." An only child, Catherine had sold her parents' house the previous year.

Eureka, once a sleepy town west of St. Louis, has grown exponentially in recent decades. Now maybe half an hour's commute by Interstate 44 to the city, it's home to many who work downtown or in growing suburbs. The town also finds itself hosting new industrial and commercial ventures. Deborah, whose father manages a large motel near Six Flags Over Missouri just to the west, lived in the new Eureka.

"She told me about a neighborhood game they used to play when she was a girl," Deborah went on. "'Up Against the Wall.' I thought she was just being nostalgic, but now . . . "

"Up Against the Wall" resembled asking what you would do if you were stuck on a deserted island: who do you want with you; if you had only one book, what is it; would you rather have plumbing facilities or clothes? These adolescent kids added the element of sexual experimentation to their version, though, making it more like Spin the Bottle or Tip the Scales.

Catherine and her friends played Up Against the Wall out in the woods where the landscape lent the game a material framework. There was a high bluff deep in one hollow about a mile's walk from town, and whoever was "it" in Up Against the Wall had to stand with his or her back against that dull face of limestone. There was nowhere to go when the questions came, and everybody had to take a turn standing up against the rock.

"They asked questions about each other," Deborah explained. "Like 'If Jimmy took a stuffed animal to bed, what animal would it be?' Or 'When Barbara takes a bath, what kind of floating toy is in the water with her?'" With some kids, this might have turned mean quickly. Catherine said her friends were always having fun.

The task for "it" was to come up with either the right answer or a funny one. If everyone could agree that Ben, first thing each morning, looked for chest hairs in the mirror, then Angie escaped from the wall. Or if the circle of friends guffawed when Sam insisted that Jackie put her brother's athletic supporter on beneath her prom dress, he didn't have to pay the penalty.

The penalty varied with each player. That was decided by the group, minus "it" and the questioner. For instance, Barbara would have to kiss Jimmy's (closed) lips, or Sam might get to put his hand in the back pocket of Dawn's jeans and pinch. Deborah didn't know how far these teasing situations went, but, again, Catherine acknowledged no anxiety from her times Up Against the Wall.

Indeed, she giggled when she admitted some of the more provocative penalties. She wouldn't give the name, though, of the girl who had to turn her back to the group and let one boy slide his hand up beneath her sweater. Nor would she identify the boy who had to lower his trousers so that a girl could give him fourteen birthday spanks.

"We were never in a hurry in those days," Catherine apparently told Deborah as they walked away from the shut-in. "We thought childhood would last forever."

"But you wouldn't want to stay a kid. Especially with all you've got right now. Aren't you flying off to Paris and Berlin on business? What you do is so exciting!"

"It is, and it isn't. Tell the truth, I feel up against the wall right now. Time is racing along, rushing me through a lifetime. In fact, I'm going to step out of the rat race for a time, perhaps forever. And I have a favor to ask of you."

"Sure, Catherine. You've done so much for me." Deborah knew that her godmother had set up a trust fund in her name and had already begun to pay her college tuition.

"See that bluff across the stream over there?" They had come to a wide clearing crossed by a quiet brook that fed the shut-in less than half a mile away. The bluff was several hundred yards away at the base of a small mountain, tree covered and steep.

"Sure."

"I'm going to walk to the bluff, turn around and wave, then disappear into the hillside."

"What?"

"Don't worry. It's perfectly OK. I'll be fine. You'll hear from me soon by postcard. I want you to tell everyone what's happened and not to worry. Just wait here and don't follow me until after I wave.

OK?" Deborah later wished she hadn't agreed. But Catherine was not a woman she was used to disobeying. Still, she has not seen her godmother since that day.

Catherine gave her hug, crossed the stream on a series of rocks, hiked to a sunny spot on the bluff. She smiled and waved. Then she turned again and stepped forward into the mountain.

Of course, there had to be a cave there, though it was never found. The authorities didn't bring in sophisticated equipment anyway, as Catherine, later the same day, reassured state police and business associates of her well-being. They might have tracked her down eventually, had any crime been asserted. But no one ever claimed that, and she left her affairs in perfect order.

She's never surfaced in her old world, though the cards she sends Deborah are all postmarked in Missouri. We can only conclude that she was up against the wall in ways the rest of us don't understand. And that the land swallowed her up in a fashion she desired. Alive and well, presumably happy in some close but out-of-the-way place, she's become another Missouri legend.

Route 66 books by Michael Lund

Growing Up on Route 66 — Michael Lund (2000) ISBN 1-888725-31-1 Novel evoking fond memories of what it was like to grow up alongside "America's Highway" in 20th Century Missouri. (Trade paperback) 5x8 260 pp,

Route 66 Kids — Michael Lund (2002) ISBN 1-888725-70-2 Sequel to *Growing Up on Route 66*, continuing memories of what it was like to grow up alongside "America's Highway" in 20th Century Missouri. (Trade paperback) 5x8 270 pp,

A Left-hander on Route 66--Michael Lund (2003) ISBN 1-888725-88-5. Twenty years after the fact, left-hander Hugh Noone appeals a wrongful conviction that detoured him from "America's Main Street" and put him in jail. But revealing the details of the past and effecting a resolution of his case mean a dramatic rearrangement of his world, including troubled relationships with three women: Linda Roy, Patty Simpson, and Karen Murphy. (Trade paperback) 5x8 270 pp,

Route 66 Spring-- Michael Lund (2004) ISBN: 1-888725-98-2. The lives of four young Missourians are changed when a bottle comes to the surface of one of the state's many natural springs. Inside is a letter written by a girl a dozen years after the end of the Civil War. Lucy Rivers Johns ' epistle contains a sad story of family failure and a powerful plea for help. This message from the last century crystallizes the individual frustrations of Janet Masters, Freddy Sills, Louis Clark, and Roberta Green, another group of

Route 66 kids. Their response to the past charts a bold path into the future, a path inspired by the Mother Road itself. (Trade paperback) 5x8 270 pp,

Miss Route 66--Michael Lund (2004) ISBN 1-888725-96-6. In the fourth novel of Michael Lund's Route 66 Novel Series, Susan Bell tells the story of her candidacy in Fairfield, Missouri's annual beauty contest. Now married and with teenage children in St. Louis, she recounts her youthful adventure in this small town along "America's Highway." At the same time, she plans a return to Fairfield in order to right injustices she feels were done to some young contestants in the Miss Route 66 Pageant. (Trade paperback) 5½ X8¼, 260 pp, **Audiobook** on 5 CD's ISBN 1-888725-12-5

Route 66 to Vietnam Michael Lund (2004) ISBN 1-59630-000-0 This novel takes characters from earlier works in the Route 66 Novel Series farther west than Los Angeles, official destination of the famous highway, Route 66. Mark Landon and Billy Rhodes find the values they grew up on challenged by America's role in Southeast Asia. But elements of their upbringing represented by the Mother Road also sustain them in ways they could never have anticipated. . (Trade paperback) 5½ X8¼, 270 pp,

AudioBook on CD—Route 66 to Vietnam ISBN: 1-59630-011-6 Michael Lund's fictional commentary from the viewpoint of a draftee. by Michael Lund unabridged 6 CD's --9 hours running time.

Route 66 Chapel Michael Lund (2006) ISBN 1-59630-012-4 Route 66 Chapel, Michael Lund (2006) (Trade paperback) 5½ X8¼, 260 pp,. When the forces of progress threaten the foundation of smalltown life—a small church—five senior citizens, a mysterious newcomer, and one young couple band together in an unlikely campaign to save it. The embattled meeting point of old and new is Route 66 Chapel, a building curiously linked to America's "Mother Road."

Route 66 Choir-- A Comedy (2010)

Michael Lund ISBN 9781596300583   284 pp 5" x 8" In Route 66 Choir Stanley Measure takes early retirement just before September 11, 2001, and his impulsive decisions participate in an unraveling of confidence in the American way of life. His wife Felicia finds that everything she holds dear is in danger of coming apart: her marriage, her church, her business, and even her country. Who or what can orchestrate the recovery of harmony necessary to sustain the spirit of the Mother Road?

   Route 66 Bride (Fall 2010)

BeachHouse Books

www.beachhousebooks.com

an Imprint of

𝔖cience & 𝔥umanities 𝔓ress
PO Box 7151
Chesterfield, MO 63006-7151

(636) 394-4950
www.beachhousebooks.com

Our books are guaranteed:

If a book has a defect, or doesn't hold up under normal use, or if you are unhappy in any way with one of our books, we are interested to know about it and will replace it and credit reasonable return shipping costs. Products with publisher defects (i.e., books with missing pages, etc.) may be returned at any time without authorization. However, we request that you describe the problem, to help us to continuously improve.

Educators Discount Policy

To encourage use of our books for education, educators can purchase three or more books (mixed titles) on our standard discount schedule for resellers. See **sciencehumanitiespress.com/educator/educator.htm l** for more detail or call Science & Humanities Press, PO Box 7151, Chesterfield MO 63006-7151636-394-4950